"YOU TORTURE ME IN MY DREAMS, DID YOU know that?" Dane said.

She gasped, then a tiny moan escaped her lips.

"And then I lie awake all night wondering things." He looked at her mouth with hunger. "What does your mouth taste like, Adria?"

She shook her head slightly.

"Is that, 'No, you don't know'? Or, 'No, don't find out'?" He rubbed his thumb over her lip. "I'm an investigator, Adria. That's what I do." He leaned down, his breath warmed her lips. "Investigate."

Just when she thought he'd end her agony and kiss her, he lifted his head slightly.

The tiniest of twinkles flickered in his eyes. "May I?"

"You'd better," she answered hoarsely.

He slid one hand to cup the side of her face, as he pulled her wrist up and placed her palm on his chest. He held it there, letting his heartbeat pulse heavily against her fingertips.

He dropped a torturously light kiss on her lips. "Remember," he warned. "I'm very thorough."

WHAT ARE *LOVESWEPT* ROMANCES?

They are stories of true romance and touching emotion. We believe those two very important ingredients are constants in our highly sensual and very believable stories in the LOVESWEPT line. Our goal is to give you, the reader, stories of consistently high quality that may sometimes make you laugh, sometimes make you cry, but are always fresh and creative and contain many delightful surprises within their pages.

Most romance fans read an enormous number of books. Those they truly love, they keep. Others may be traded with friends and soon forgotten. We hope that each LOVE-SWEPT romance will be a treasure—a "keeper." We will always try to publish

LOVE STORIES YOU'LL NEVER FORGET
BY AUTHORS YOU'LL ALWAYS REMEMBER

The Editors

THE THREE MUSKETEERS: MIDNIGHT HEAT

DONNA KAUFFMAN

BANTAM BOOKS
NEW YORK · TORONTO · LONDON · SYDNEY · AUCKLAND

THE THREE MUSKETEERS: MIDNIGHT HEAT
A Bantam Book / February 1996

ISBN 0-553-44472-7

Published simultaneously in the United States and Canada

Bantam Books are published by Bantam Books, a division of Bantam Dou-
bleday Dell Publishing Group, Inc. Its trademark, consisting of the words
"Bantam Books" and the portrayal of a rooster, is Registered in U.S.
Patent and Trademark Office and in other countries. Marca Registrada.
Bantam Books, 1540 Broadway, New York, New York 10036.

PRINTED IN THE UNITED STATES OF AMERICA

OPM   0 9 8 7 6 5 4 3 2 1

ACKNOWLEDGMENTS

I would like to thank the air-traffic controllers and National Transportation Safety Board investigators who were so generous with their time and expertise in helping me with the overwhelming task of researching this book. Please accept my apologies for the oversimplification and creative license I've taken with the actual functions of your jobs for the sake of this fictional story. The work you do is demanding and so very important. You have my eternal gratitude.

DEDICATION

I would like to dedicate this book to the one person without whom this book would not only have not been written, but never conceived. To my sister-in-law, Amy, who has an encyclopedic knowledge of air-traffic control and aviation. You always wanted an ATC story, now you have one! I learned some fascinating (and frightening) things while writing this book. I imagine the only thing you learned was never again to make suggestions about this neat story idea you have.

AUTHOR'S NOTE

When my editor called to tell me she thought that Loveswept's annual Treasured Tales would be the perfect way to celebrate the grand finale of my *The Three Musketeers* trilogy, I was flattered and excited. When Loveswept first launched this theme month several years ago, I knew it would be a smash hit. I mean, what better way to spend a few hours than exploring a favorite fantasy retold by some of the best romance writers in the business? Having been only one of the many to read them each year, I can say with total certainty that . . . I was right!

And now I get to be a part of it!

My first reaction was to pump my fist in the air and say a heartfelt *yes!* My second reaction, which lasted much longer, was, "Oh, no, *I'm* going to write a Treasured Tale?" Panic set in. Then my editor gently reminded me that this particular story really captured the magic of *The Three Musketeers*, a passionate tale of heroes who put it all on the line in the name of honor, loyalty, and most of all, love. This story already was a Treasured Tale.

And I realized that it was for exactly those reasons that I had proposed this series in the first place. So, I'm honored—and thrilled—to have MIDNIGHT HEAT take its place on the shelves with the other fables, myths, and stories of old made new once again. Now you have only to turn the page to discover how, once upon a time, my last musketeer, the man who has always prided himself on his perfect control, loses it to one very cool damsel in distress.

Happy swashbuckling!

Donna Kauffman

Donna Kauffman

ONE

The Predator was coming. For her.

Adria Burke had heard the whispers over an hour ago as she sat in the small airless office deep in the bowels of Washington, D.C.'s, Metropolitan Airport.

The Predator. The National Transportation Safety Board investigator Dane Colbourne. The man who never left a case unsolved. The man now assigned to cover "the incident."

Her incident.

Adria watched the hour hand four. Four *A.M.* She huffe shifted her gaze to the co tom of her cup. She i wanted dregs. Oth times heated dis

Mark Beck, she hadn't spoken to a soul since midnight.

"Where is this guy?"

It was at least the hundredth time she'd wondered it, but the first time she'd said it out loud. The sound of her own voice, tired and scratchy, did little to boost her morale.

She'd reviewed in exacting detail her role in the midair collision that had taken place shortly after she'd assumed her position in the control tower. And each time she'd come to the same conclusion: It wasn't her fault. If she were faced with the same horrifying scenario again, she'd make the same decisions, issue the same commands. That the two pilots, their crews, and passengers had somehow come out of it safely had been a miracle.

But that a major disaster had been averted was not the issue. Two planes had collided, and now she was under investigation. If Dane Col- ne reached the conclusion that she was she'd likely pay the price of being

nsidered her assignment to nal and professional vic- he'd fought so hard, af- been through . . . e.

night. And then bye. Unless she er side of the

story. Beck hadn't wanted to hear about the fact that up until seconds before the Liberty and AirWest planes collided, there had been a third plane—a primary target—on her display, in the same area as the other two planes. A plane whose direction and speed had decided her on her course of action.

Where in hell had that damn plane come from? And more important, where had it gone? It had simply disappeared from her display. And why wouldn't anyone believe her?

That the last man she had a shot at convincing was referred to in awed whispers as the Predator only increased the dull throbbing in her temples.

She looked to the door, willing it to open. Willing the man she was waiting for to enter.

She treated her tired mind to the pleasure of imagining what Colbourne must look like. Over fifty, beady eyes, thinning hair hel place with Brylcreem. Short, stock attitude problem. Anal-retentive was probably ex-military, the gravel for breakfast, then who got in his path the

Jack Nicholson's f "Ooooh, the Pre mock horror.

That very i Choking b

up into her throat, Adria stared in shock at the man who entered the room.

So much for over fifty. He couldn't be much older than her own thirty-one. Short was definitely out as well; he was easily six feet, with well-distributed muscles. She didn't catch his eyes as he passed, so beady was still a possibility. What she did see of his face was all strong, clean angles. Now she understood what chiseled features meant. His hair wasn't oily or thinning. It was thick, wavy, and light brown, cut razor sharp in a way that enhanced the chiseled look.

But it wasn't any of those things that had her jaw dropping.

It was the crisp, white, perfectly tailored tuxedo with tails he was wearing.

Any hope she'd had of regaining her composure fled when he stopped at a metal desk turned around. His cummerbund was a bright fuchsia. She had no idea where a rose to match. But there was one, white satin lapel.

Predator?

trained herself from asking let him leave the dream

ers onto the desk. lled it out, and e sat. He said e contents of the top file. He had yet to look in her direction.

Irritation crowded out Adria's surprise. Well, she hadn't been completely skunked. She'd apparently hit the bull's-eye on his severe attitude problem. And from the arrow-straight back and perfectly squared shoulders to the neatly piled folders, she bet she wasn't too far off on the anal-retentive assessment either. Even his rose hadn't wilted.

Although he probably wouldn't appreciate her concern, she took a second and tried to dredge up some sympathy for him. He'd obviously been dragged away from some important function. She half wondered if it wasn't his own wedding. That wouldn't surprise her in the least.

A full minute passed and still no sign that he was aware of her. She sighed in disgust. If he'd thought to ambush her with his getup and intimidate her with his silent treatment, then he was in for a rude surprise. She'd learned that game at the feet of a master.

She stood and held out her hand. "Mr. Colbourne, I presume?"

No response came while he continued his silent study. Adria felt the heat of anger climb into her cheeks. Unwise words were on the very tip of her tongue when he finally spoke.

"Sorry to keep you waiting," he said, not

looking up or sounding the least bit sorry. In fact, there was no emotion in his voice at all.

She was sorely tempted to ask him if he always conducted his interrogations in formal wear, just to see if she could get a reaction—any reaction—out of him. The impulse was instantly forgotten when he suddenly raised his head and looked directly at her for the first time.

"You can take a seat, Ms. Burke. This will probably take a while."

Adria's still-proffered hand dropped to her side while she stared at his eyes. Hazel. A muted green with just a hint of gold. Faintly bloodshot, with little fatigue lines at the corners. All in all, not the kind of eyes that should warrant any special attention.

So why did they capture hers?

A shiver tickled her spine. She had the odd sensation that he was testing her. She felt . . . well, the only word she could think of was pinned. And she really hated it.

He dipped his chin, his gaze flicking to the chair behind her. "I'm ready to begin."

The reality of the situation hit her. He was calling the shots. He was also her last hope. She'd learned the value of asserting herself, but she hadn't forgotten that timing was everything. And now wasn't the time. So she merely nodded, then sat down.

"I'd like to ask you some specific questions

about your actions immediately after taking control of your position."

She swallowed hard against the almost desperate need to blurt out her view of the night's events, forcing him to listen and believe. She'd tried that with Beck and had gotten nowhere. Instead, she curled her fingers into fists, then slowly, purposefully relaxed them. A stress-management technique she'd mastered during her divorce. Or precisely, *en*during. Studiously avoiding the Predator's attire, she focused on a point between his eyes and blanked her own expression to match his.

"Ask away," she said, proud of the steady tone.

"I understand that shortly after taking control of your position last night, you issued an altitude change to Liberty Flight 576. Is that correct?"

"Yes, it's correct." She didn't mention the fact that Pete Moore, the controller who held the shift before her, had left the plane dangerously close to the AirWest plane. "There was a third plane—" she continued on.

"Please, Ms. Burke," he interrupted. "Just answer my questions yes or no for the time being."

Of all the . . . Stay cool. Stay calm. One benefit of being an air-traffic controller was the conditioned response to high-stress situations. This certainly qualified.

Adding control freak to her mental description list of the Predator, she clenched her teeth and said, "Yes, sir."

He held her gaze for an interminable second, then dropped it back to the notes. "The Liberty pilot reports you then issued a radar warning about a primary target, followed by new coordinates and another change in altitude."

"Yes."

"You then issued new coordinates to the AirWest pilot, after which the pilot received a TCAS warning," he said, referring to the Traffic Collision Avoidance System, a mechanism onboard each aircraft. "You countermanded that warning due to the supposed involvement of the primary target."

She remained silent.

After a long while he gave her a hard look. "Ms. Burke?"

"Yes?" Adria blamed exhaustion for her irrational need to bring him down a notch. But really, the situation was tense enough without his attitude filling up the room.

"You have no response?"

"Yes, I do. But you didn't ask me a direct yes-or-no question. I was simply trying to follow orders. Sir."

A scowl began to form in his mouth. Adria couldn't suppress the pleasure she took in that tiny victory. So, he could feel an emotion after all. Even if it was irritation.

The Predator tossed his pencil on the desk and leaned back in his chair. "It's been a long night, Ms. Burke. I really don't have the patience to sit here and play games with you."

Adria imagined he had unlimited patience. Most hunters did.

"My goal here," he continued, "is determining the cause of the incident. I have an AirWest pilot who says he responded to your directions after the TCAS, only to scrape wingtips with the Liberty, causing both pilots to temporarily lose control of their aircrafts. I don't have to tell you the odds they beat in getting safely to the ground."

"And I'm telling you my coordinates were correct," she shot back, then paused a moment. "Actually, Mr. Colbourne, I've gone over this and over this." Her voice was more controlled, but the electric intensity underlying each word betrayed the cost. "And I don't think the Liberty and the AirWest did connect."

"So just what do you think they did collide with?" he demanded. "A UFO?"

"Not in the way you mean, no." She hurried on before he could comment. "As unbelievable as it may sound, I think they both clipped the primary target."

He simply continued to stare at her. "Let's

say for the moment that your . . . scenario is possible." His flat tone indicated what he thought of that possibility. "If the primary target had clipped tips with the other planes, it would most certainly have lost control as well, if not crashed. We have no indication of that happening. At the very least, someone on board the Liberty or the AirWest would have seen the primary target if it was as close as you said in your report."

"There was dense cloud cover, not to mention the fact that it was the middle of the night," she responded immediately. "So any sight reports would be suspect."

He leaned forward and rested his elbows on the desk. Why did she get the impression that he was going in for the kill?

"Before you dig yourself in any deeper, Ms. Burke, perhaps you should be aware that both of the captains and their first officers aren't completely convinced that the primary target ever existed."

Dane Colbourne watched her closely. Surprise, then anger showed openly on her face. But not even a flicker of fear or vulnerability. He didn't know what to make of her.

She shot to her feet and planted her fists on the edge of the desk. "What do you mean they don't think there was a third plane?" Her shoulder-length brown hair swung forward with the abrupt movement, her eyes shone bright with indignation. They were blue, he now realized. A clear, brilliant blue, like the sky at twenty thousand feet. "Of course there was a third plane! It sure as hell was on my display! Check the tapes if you have to. But it was there. And it must have flown right between the Liberty and the AirWest."

If it hadn't happened hours ago, Dane would have questioned whether or not those few glasses of champagne he'd had at his sister Dara's wedding reception had actually impaired his thinking. Her theory was crazy. And he'd have to be crazy to believe it. But his thinking wasn't impaired. And one thing he was very clear about was that when it came to one Ms. Adria Burke, nothing she said or did was going to be taken lightly.

Damn but he wanted some aspirin. Raking a hand through his hair, he worked harder for a patient tone than he could remember having to do for some time. One look at the stubborn set to her jaw told him that even if he dredged it up, it wasn't likely to hold for long.

"Your theory leaves too much unexplained," he said shortly.

Adria rolled her eyes and made a very unladylike sound of disgust. And Dane suddenly—impossibly—found himself fighting the urge to smile. He was used to mowing people down with his confidence and certainty, used to getting the job done and done right. Only now did he realize just how exhilarating a worthy adversary might be. If this wasn't so serious, he might actually enjoy going head to head with her.

She blew out a deep breath, causing the wispy hair fringing her forehead to flutter up, then settle down in complete disarray.

He watched her, waiting and wondering what she'd do or say next. Wondering why he felt such an odd sense of anticipation. Why in the hell he didn't step in and bring this to his customary finality with a few well-chosen, completely unchallengeable statements.

"Listen," she said finally. Didn't she know just how completely she had his attention? "I don't see why we're even arguing about this. I mean, the ARTS III tapes contain all the display data. They'll prove what was there. That the third plane *was* there."

She really was amazing, he thought. She'd been through a harrowing experience, and while the ending had ultimately been a happy one for the passengers and crew, her job was still on the line. She had to be wiped out. And yet she sat there and defended her actions in a rational and calm manner.

Well, mostly calm anyway. He lowered his head and scanned his notes again, stifling for the second time the urge to smile.

He'd looked at her job file and had to admit he was very impressed. She'd passed her written test on the first try, which wasn't so unusual, but her scores had been perfect. Then she'd been one of the lucky ones to pass her security clearance check quickly and had landed a plum—and highly unusual—assignment straight out. She'd obtained her FPL— full performance level—rating there in what had to be record time. It normally took four years, she'd done it in three. And the fairy-tale career had continued when her first FPL assignment had been a level-five facility. D.C.'s Metropolitan.

Any suspicions about how she might have landed it would have been put to rest by her work record. She'd been here two years and her performance rating was outstanding. Until recently. It was that tiny section of her work history that he'd focused on. Had to focus on.

According to her file, she'd been reprimanded twice in the last six months. Neither time for anything remotely as serious as the collision, and both times she'd shouldered the blame entirely with no argument, no excuses offered.

Even now, it seemed to him she was as concerned with determining what really happened as she was with clearing her name. His strengths as an investigator were the same ones she'd obviously developed as a controller.

The ability to remain cool and detached no matter how extreme the circumstances. To focus on the facts at hand.

In his case that included going over and over every detail of an incident until any flaw in logic or action was uncovered and analyzed. And all the cold hard facts in this case—not to mention the flaws—pointed at the controller sitting directly across from him.

He couldn't ignore the regret he felt, but he didn't let it come through when he spoke. "They are making copies of the ARTS tapes as we speak. The data printout will include everything from the time you took over control of your position. I'll also be going over the voice and data tapes from both flights."

He stood and massaged the bridge of his nose, his headache having settled into a slow steady throb. "I will probably have additional questions. Please leave a number with Mr. Beck where you can be reached, and try to stay accessible."

Several moments of silence passed, then she stood. "That's it?" she asked with disbelief.

Not hardly, he wanted to respond, but didn't. Dane swallowed a groan as his shoulder and neck muscles began to compete with the pain in his head. He had long hours ahead of him with no sleep in sight. Instead of the usual rush of anticipation he felt when he took on a new investigation, he simply felt tired. And confused. He never felt confused.

"I'm very thorough, Ms. Burke." He locked gazes with her once more. "And I'm damn good. I'll find out what happened. No matter what."

She opened her mouth as if to speak, but only huffed out a small sigh of resignation. It bothered Dane more than he cared to admit just how curious he was to know what she'd been about to say.

She lifted her purse from the chair and dug inside. Pulling out a small pad and pencil, she hastily scribbled something, then tore the sheet off and handed it to him. "My home phone number," she told him. "Though as thorough as you are, I'm sure you have it there in those notes somewhere. As you probably also know, I'm not union, so I've been placed on temporary leave until you file your report with Mr. Beck and the FAA. There's a machine on that line in case I'm not home."

She was such an easy read. He knew she was dying to ask what his early conclusions were. But she wasn't going to. Even though she understood that whatever final decision was made would be done largely on the basis of his report. He was very probably holding her entire career in his hands. A career that, up until just recently, she'd obviously worked damn hard to make a stellar one. He couldn't deny that he admired her silence.

It wasn't until he tried to tuck the card in the inside pocket of his jacket that he remembered he was still wearing his tuxedo.

When he'd been beeped at the reception, the only phone available had been in the limo that had brought some of the wedding party. Once he'd called in and been briefed, his only concern had been getting to the airport. He hadn't taken the time to go home or even drop in at his office to change.

He caught a glimmer of humor in her eyes before she carefully masked it.

"I, uh, was at a wedding reception. My sister's," he said, wondering even as he offered the explanation why he'd done so. He wasn't used to explaining himself, preferring to let his work speak for him. That he hadn't, until this moment, given any thought to how people perceived him on a personal level did little to ease his uncustomary awkwardness. When she didn't say anything, he felt foolish. He stuffed the card into the top folder. "I'll let you know if I find out anything to support your theory."

"Thank you," was all she said. Clearly she didn't think he was going to look too hard for that support. That rankled. But he'd be damned if he'd offer any further assurances. She'd learn about him soon enough.

Then a spark of something he couldn't put

a name to flashed in her eyes. "Nice tux." She reached out to straighten his rose. "Hot pink is definitely your color." Then she turned and left the room without another word.

The back of his neck grew warm with embarrassment, but it was the idea that she didn't expect him to help her that stuck in his mind. Why? He was her main if not only chance of exoneration. Was she the sort that didn't rely on others? Did she always fight her own battles? If so, why hadn't she defended herself on her past two reprimands? She didn't strike him as the kind to take anything silently. Was the Adria Burke he'd dealt with tonight the rule, or the exception?

Another mystery for him to solve. If he wanted to.

And he discovered he did.

He shook his head. Crazy thoughts. Crazy night. Maybe it was just some strange reaction after watching his twin sister marry one of only two people in the world he'd ever gotten close to. He was still having a hard time adjusting to the fact that Zach Brogan, his childhood buddy, was now his brother-in-law. Jarrett McCullough, the other member of their childhood trio, had tied the knot just over a month ago. Now Dane was the last of the Three Musketeers left single. And he couldn't escape the fact that it left him feeling oddly, irrationally, abandoned.

As adults, the three had gone their separate ways, but had never been truly apart. Not in the ways that counted. Months would pass when he didn't know where either of them were, but he was certain that, no matter what, they'd be there for him when it counted. Just as he'd always be there for them no matter what.

Dane sighed and headed to the door. Part of him, the rational part he'd always relied on, knew that their recent marriages wouldn't change that fact.

But the other part, the emotional one, the part he rarely acknowledged and only then when he was forced to, wasn't sure of anything right now.

"Ah hell," he muttered. Maybe Dara was right. Maybe he just needed to get laid.

But as he picked up the phone to call a cab for a ride over to his office in L'Enfant Plaza, he couldn't help but wonder if what he really needed was to get a life.

TWO

The phone rang just as Adria pulled the bandanna off of her head and mopped her face and neck. The late-summer humidity made the air feel almost liquid. She brushed the dirt from her knees and dug her knuckles into the knot in her lower back as she dashed into the house.

She was more out of shape than she'd thought if a short jog to the house was winding her. And if the sorry shape of her garden could be used as a measuring stick of how often she got out, she'd been out of shape for some time.

Maybe it was Pete Moore calling her to finally express gratitude for the flak she'd taken for him twice. He hadn't been too happy with her after their little talk yesterday. He was so wrapped up in the misery of going through a divorce, nothing much was getting past the thick fog of his self-pity.

Then again, Pete hadn't asked for her help, she admitted. *She* had hurt for Pete, feeling all the pain she'd felt during her own divorce.

Skidding to a stop beside the kitchen counter, she scooped up the receiver on the fourth ring. Her voice was a bit breathless as she said, "Hello?"

There was a pause, then a deep voice said, "Ms. Burke?"

Her heart beat faster and her hand tightened on the receiver. It wasn't Pete.

It was the man she'd last seen almost two days before in a small office. Two days. Forty-eight hours. Not very long really. Unless you were used to working fourteen- or fifteen-hour days.

"Yes, it is." She took a moment to steady her nerves. "Mr. Colbourne?"

"Yes." One word, bitten off so sharply she wondered if she should check her ear for blood. The man was not happy. So what else was new?

"What can I do for you?"

"You can stop talking to the media, that's what you can do."

"What?" For the second time in as many meetings, he'd caught her completely off guard. "What are you talking about?"

"I'm talking about the story on the investigation, *my* investigation. Page four, first section, *Washington Post*, early edition." He hadn't raised his voice, but his dark tone fairly vibrated.

"I don't take the *Post*," she stated, more calmly than he deserved. "And I have no idea what you are talking about."

"You're telling me you aren't the 'inside source' quoted in the piece?"

"That's exactly what I'm telling you. So go hunt down someone else, this time I'm blame-free."

The silence lasted only a second, but the sense of foreboding carried over the line with ease. "This time?"

Adria shivered at his accusatory tone. "We all make mistakes, Mr. Colbourne, and I've got a list probably longer than most. But negligence isn't on there." She put special emphasis on that last part. "I was speaking in generalities." Before he could remark, she added, "Instead of giving me a hard time because some reporter is dogging you, why aren't you out there finding out what in the hell happened to that third plane?"

"Funny you should mention that."

"And here I thought you didn't have a sense of humor." The retort was out before she could think to stop it.

"Ms. Burke, I'd like to see you in my office this afternoon. Before five if possible."

Yes, master. "Am I permitted to ask why?" She tried hard to keep the sarcasm out of her voice, knowing she'd baited him enough. Too much, considering the role he was playing in her bid to keep her career. Two days at home—gardening!—had taken a huge toll on her.

"The newspaper article is only part of a bigger problem. I think it would be better discussed in person. Let me give you directions."

Adria swallowed the half-dozen questions that sprang immediately to mind, knowing there was no point in asking him now. "I know where your building is located, just tell me where in the building you are." She went on, without letting him speak. "And it will be at least five. I'm all sweaty from . . . well, never mind. It'll take me a while to get there. By the time I get out of here, traffic will be impossible."

Silence. And this time she couldn't fathom why. But the reason didn't feel like anger. So softly she barely heard it, he slowly expelled a long breath. She shivered again, but this time chill was not a factor. And the heat was strictly internal.

It wasn't as if he were asking for a date, she told herself, rubbing her arms. God knows the man always sounded absorbed and busy, not flirtatious. Tense, focused, determined, single-minded. Yes, she already knew Dane Colbourne was all of those things. Not in her wildest dreams could she picture a man so self-contained being playful.

But the man had dark and seductive nailed right to the wall. Even if he didn't know it.

It was just as well this *was* business. She'd stick with her harmless fantasies. No one ever got hurt from exerting a little imagination.

And yet, perversely, she couldn't help but wonder what he did for pleasure. Or where. Maybe imagination wasn't as harmless as she thought. Not when the fantasy involved Dane Colbourne.

"I'll be here," he said finally. There was the slightest trace of fatigue in his voice, but even that vanished as he quickly issued succinct directions. "Did you get all that?"

She'd gotten about half of it. He hadn't waited for her to get a pen. No way was she asking him to repeat himself. "Yes," she answered, then couldn't help adding, "Is the dress code for this meeting formal? Or will casual be okay?"

This time the silence extended long enough to give her plenty of time to kick herself for not learning to curb her impulses around him. Then a weird sound carried over the line, sort of throaty and a bit rusty.

No. He couldn't have actually laughed. A reluctant smile tugged at her lips. One emotion Dane Colbourne didn't inspire in her was boredom.

"Not tonight," he said finally, the faintest trace of dry humor in his voice. "My tux is at the cleaners. Casual will have to do."

A short laugh escaped before she could stifle it. He was almost tolerable when he tried. "You know, Colbourne, there just might be some hope for you yet." She was more than a little disturbed by the throaty sound of her voice when she added, "And please, call me Adria."

She hung up before he could reply.

Dane swore as he finally shut the folder he'd been making notes in. He looked at his watch—something he'd sworn he wasn't going to do just five minutes before—then swore again. It was almost five-thirty. "Where the hell is she?"

Very likely stuck on the Beltway in rush-hour traffic. God only knew what sort of mood she'd be in by the time she arrived. Not that he cared. This was business after all, not a date.

He hoped her car had air-conditioning.

He downed the rest of his Coke, pitched it into the recycling trash can already overflowing with empties, then unburied his notebook, sliding the wrinkled paper with her number from the inside flap.

He didn't need it anymore. The number had been committed to memory long before he'd even been aware of repeatedly looking at it.

The sound of her voice when she'd first answered the phone played through his mind again. He'd been so frustrated. Hell, he'd been full-blown angry when he'd dialed her number. But the first sound of her voice, all heated and breathless, and he'd found himself struggling to remember why.

And just when he'd worked up a good head of indignant steam, she'd tossed off that comment about being all hot and sweaty, then had deliberately trailed off from the why of it. Leaving his mind soaring over the possibilities, none of them improving his mood and all of them creating a little sweat on his own usually cool brow.

Damn but the woman tied him in knots.

He dug into the small cooler he kept under his desk, but instead of pulling out a fresh can, he grabbed a couple of ice cubes and popped them in his mouth. He purposely let them sit there until his tongue began to go numb. Numb. That's what he wanted to be around her. What he needed to be. Detached, remote, emotionally uninvolved. All the things that he'd perfected—had to perfect in order to do his job—had vanished the moment she reached up and straightened his boutonniere.

And this afternoon she'd actually hung up on him.

"Mr. Colbourne?"

Dane almost choked on the ice cubes. Adria was standing in the doorway to his office. She was wearing a loose flowery print dress with a neckline that covered way too much and short little sleeves that didn't cover anything. A tiny ribbon, barely cinched, emphasized the difference between her waist and her hips. The dress material was filmy enough to give a glimpse of her long, lean frame. Life truly wasn't fair. He wanted to groan.

"You call that casual?" He couldn't believe he'd just said that.

Her polite smile faltered briefly, then she nodded toward his chest, where his neatly knotted tie rested. Framed by his suit jacket. "I figured this was a safe compromise."

She hadn't compromised a thing, he thought, wanting to look away, knowing he should.

And he was beginning to understand there wasn't a damn thing safe about her.

She entered his office and did a slow study of his cramped surroundings. He followed her gaze. His office was small, windowless, functional, and decorated in early government issue. Gray metal desk, gray-and-black metal file cabinets—as many as he could cram in—functional swivel chair, one long folding table littered with pieces of various planes, most tagged, some not, stacks of black cardboard boxes crammed with files, and two metal wastebaskets. One overflowing with paper, the other with Coke cans.

That last item raised her eyebrows.

"My one addiction." He was disturbed to discover that explaining himself was rapidly becoming a habit with her.

"And I would have thought your job was your only addiction."

Her lips fascinated him. Full, but not too full. Deep pink without being too pink. He enjoyed watching them move. Without thinking, he answered, "No, work is my salvation. Different thing all together."

Her eyes held a wealth of understanding. "Yes, that it is."

Dane wanted to ask her what her work had saved her from, but he was too unsettled by his own admission to ask. When she picked up an altitude indicator on his desk, he automatically reached to take it from her. "Be careful with that. It's—"

"An altimeter." She turned it over to look at the back before gently replacing it on his desk. "From a DC-3, right?"

He dropped his hand, feeling awkward and not liking it in the least. "Right." He'd be damned if he'd ask her how she knew.

"Quite a keepsake," she said. "When did they stop making them—1945?"

Dane sighed. "Forty-six."

Before he could tell her to have a seat, she picked up the sheared-off gearshift he used for a paperweight. "What investigation yielded this treasure?"

Dane curled his fingers into his palms. He felt like a kid who didn't want his stuff touched. And, also like a kid, he felt defensive about what he chose to collect.

But what he sensed in her was genuine interest. Not the mocking taunt or, worse, the guarded wariness that indicated his visitor had decided he was some sort of sicko who actually enjoyed picking through wreckage. Which was why he'd made the decision long ago to be very sure that the women in his life—when there were any—didn't come anywhere near his office or anything directly involving his professional life.

The heat that curled in his chest, the instant understanding that he could share this part of himself with her—and like it—hit him low and hard.

The investigation, he reminded himself. She's not here for your personal pleasure.

But oh how he wanted her to be.

"The runway collision three years ago in Denver," he answered her, his abrupt tone not inviting further discussion. She took the hint and put the gearshift back on his desk. He opened his mouth to ask her to take a seat, relieved to be back on track and in control. So it was a little disconcerting to hear himself ask, "Where did you learn so much about parts that you know what sort of plane they come from? Do you fly?"

She sat across from him, looking too fresh and graceful on the hard metal folding chair. She was the brightest thing this office had ever seen. Who needed windows?

"No," she said. "But my grandfather did. So did my dad."

"Mine too," he answered, shocking himself. He didn't talk about his father, not so much as a passing mention, with *anyone*. Not even Dara.

"Actually, my father wasn't a pilot by profession, not like Grandpa," she said with affection. "Dad flew for the military in the Korean conflict, then, like so many other military pilots, he was recruited by the FAA into being a controller."

"Ah," Dane said, glad to keep the conversation focused on her. "Like father, like daughter."

Her expression briefly clouded, confounding Dane. "Something like that," she said quietly. It was clear to him that sharing time was over.

Which was good. This wasn't a social call. But it didn't stop him from feeling uncomfortable, as if he should apologize for bringing up—however unintentionally—memories that were obviously bittersweet. Nor did it stop him from wanting to find out what had made them bitter and which ones were sweet.

Dane quickly turned the discussion to work, deliberately excluding his emotions from involvement. It was a skill he'd perfected early on after watching the destructive effects on coworkers when they became emotionally involved in cases that usually involved multiple fatalities. He hadn't known exactly when this detachment had become second nature. He'd never had cause to question it.

That it required more work than usual to achieve just now only made him more determined to accomplish it.

"I went over our copies of the printouts from the ARTS tapes." He ignored with great difficulty the tug in his chest that felt too much like remorse for what he was about to do to her. "According to the data, the primary was never on your display."

"I know what I saw, Mr. Colbourne," she insisted. "The plane was there. Maybe you didn't go back far enough in the data retrieval."

Mr. Colbourne. He supposed it was foolish to regret that he'd never get to hear her say his first name now.

"I went back to the beginning of your shift. All the data from the moment you took over your control, up to the moment the incident occurred is in this printout." He slid the white sheet of paper over to her.

Dane watched her as she quickly scanned the information detailed neatly—and indisputably—on the display copy he'd already memorized. The color slowly drained from her face until all that was left were two bright red spots on her cheeks.

"The plane was there," she repeated, but with only a trace of her former conviction. "What about the voice tapes?"

Dane sighed. He was hating this more than he'd expected. He doubted very much that she was liking this either.

"The voice tapes prove you tried to open communication with a primary target and that you warned the AirWest and Liberty pilots of its approach," he said.

"And doesn't that count for anything? I mean, why would I have done that if it wasn't there?"

Disappointment had no place in this investigation, Dane reminded himself harshly. "I'm not saying you didn't *think* you saw something.

But the bottom line is the ARTS tapes don't back you up."

She handed the paper back to him. He'd braced himself for and expected to see defeat in those sky-blue eyes. But for once, his instincts failed him.

For some reason, he wasn't too disappointed by that.

She stood and pressed her fists on his desk. "There has to be some other way I can prove my theory."

"There is no eyewitness, not one, who can state categorically that they saw a third plane." Dane massaged his stomach, then realizing what he was doing, picked up his pencil again.

Adria leaned across the desk. Dane didn't know which impulse was stronger; the one telling him to lean away in case she tried to strangle him. Or the one urging him to move closer and risk getting burned.

"Then you don't have any real proof that my explanation is wrong either. Do you?" The last part had been issued as pure challenge. But she didn't wait to see whether he'd take her up on it. She spun away and began to pace. Her long legs made short work of it and she quit after several rounds, abruptly stopping to lean against the narrow table that ran along the wall across from his desk.

Her gaze became a little unfocused.

Dane remained silent, unable—and frankly

unwilling—to conquer his immediate and complete fascination with her unpredictable actions.

He noticed the way her eyebrows pulled together and tiny lines creased her forehead as she considered and discarded whatever scenarios were rolling through her mind.

Dane respected agile minds and quick, logical thinking. But he wasn't entirely sure it was admiration of her deductive-reasoning skills that had him so attentive. He found himself wondering what spending time with her—without the interference of work—would be like. What it would be like to have that sharp intellect of hers focused solely on him. The sudden impulse to find out was overwhelmingly strong.

And just as impossible.

But there was no denying she'd captured his full attention. His dates, when he found time for them, had long ago fallen into the category of functional rather than fun. An escort to the opera in exchange for pleasant company to some NTSB function. Some evenings ended at the door, some did not. But none of them stood out in his mind as being particularly memorable.

He wondered, if they were asked, if the women would remember him either. Probably not. That's why he chose them. Why they chose him. Lately, there had been no choosing at all.

Work had been his entire life lately. But he didn't want that right now. What he wanted was Adria Burke. Would she let herself be chosen? By any man? By him?

And the hell of it was, he'd never know.

"So," she said finally, "does this mean the investigation is closed?"

Half of him wanted to ask her what possibilities she'd been mulling over while the other half wished she'd taken longer doing it. He enjoyed watching her. Couldn't remember if he'd ever actually taken pleasure in simply staring at a woman.

"No, it isn't." He could have said more, could have told her that the remaining information and data to be collected would likely continue to prove her guilt before it would exonerate her, but he didn't.

She casually lifted a block of windshield from a 727 off the table next to her, then turned the piece over and around in her hands.

"Why did the newspaper story bother you?"

Her question pulled him fully back into the matter. "Most of the story was general coverage of the collision and details on any injuries, speculation as to the cause."

"Was my name mentioned?" Her tone was

even, but strain was evident in the tightness around her mouth.

"No. Other than mentioning that an unnamed controller had been put on temporary leave, the reporter stated our standard comment that a routine investigation into the matter was ongoing."

She waited a beat, then said, "And? But? I hear at least one of those coming."

His mouth twitched, but he controlled it. She had the damnedest effect on him. "But said reporter ended her routine piece with the line 'an inside source has hinted that there may be more to this than simple navigational error.'"

Her eyes narrowed. "And you immediately thought I'd talked to the media and given them my version of the story. Given them the third plane."

Dane wasn't sure what he should feel at her accusation, but he was pretty damn sure it shouldn't be guilt. "If you thought your version would get more coverage by leaking it to the press, well then—"

"I was asked not to discuss the events of that night while the investigation is ongoing and I haven't. I understand and happen to agree with that policy. Things get distorted enough."

"It's my job to question everything, Adria." Her eyes widened at his use of her name. Her reaction set off one of his own, and he had to fight to keep his mind open and unbiased. He looked down at his notes. They didn't have accusing blue eyes.

"I'm sorry."

His head shot up. He'd been thinking those very words and for a split second wondered if he'd actually said them.

"You're right," she said. "I don't know what I expected from you."

"I think you made it clear that first night in my office you didn't expect me to do much of anything. Least of all, to help you."

She didn't deny it. "Which is why you thought I'd taken things into my own hands and approached the press. But don't you think if I had come forward, my name would be all over the place? Or at the least the third-plane scenario would have been run through the media wringer."

"Anonymous sources are most reporters' bread and butter. They wouldn't betray them. She still got her byline."

"So who did tip them off? And what else could the 'inside source' have been referring to if not the third plane." Her gaze had gone all unfocused again as she began to run through the possibilities, but suddenly she focused on him. From the sparks he saw, Dane knew her conclusion wasn't going to thrill him.

"Unless there is something else going on

here that I don't know about." She paused, then asked, "Is there any point in my even asking you?" Then her tone turned more bitter. "Or am I being incredibly naive to believe the head investigator would simply hand that sort of information over to his lead suspect?"

Dane didn't say anything. He didn't know what *to* say. Why did the idea of telling her everything not seem the terrible mistake logic dictated it would be? Instinct versus logic. Head versus heart. He was beginning to resent how easily she managed to put him in turmoil.

He turned his attention away from her and pulled another Coke from the cooler by his feet. He lifted it to her. "Thirsty?"

She shook her head. It was clear she was waiting for him to respond.

I'm responding, lady, he thought darkly as his body tightened. For the first time in a while, a very long while—maybe ever—his mind was as actively engaged as his hormones. And that was what made her so dangerous.

The lady expected answers. Even if they weren't the ones she wanted to hear.

Dane admired that. He popped the top and downed half the can. He looked back at her, waiting for the burn of the fizz to pass from his throat to his stomach. Maybe a little carbonation would settle it down. Who was he kidding?

"First, I can't tell you everything that's going on in this investigation. It isn't procedure." He held up his hand when she rolled her eyes. "Procedures, I might add, that are in place for a good reason. You know you are the main focus here. But until my report is filed, you have the right to be protected too."

"And just what is it I'm being protected from? The truth?"

"No." Dane raked his hand through his hair. "Listen, I'd like to believe you. But whether or not I do has no bearing on how thorough a job I do. I'm not in the habit of explaining myself, so you'll have to take it on faith. I don't file my report until all the facts are in. *All* of them. Neat, tidy, and no questions. That's how I like my cases. That way nothing comes back to haunt you."

Memories poured through his mind—of his father's crash, the investigators who had crawled all over the wreckage, looking at every scrap for clues. That they had determined his father hadn't been at fault had been Dane's only solace at a time when nothing in his life made sense. He'd understood right then the power of fact, of the tangible. And the very high risk of faith and trust. Not to mention love.

The fire in her gentled to something more warm, more soothing. She stepped to his desk. "Dane, listen, I—"

Dane. Damn if his name on her lips didn't

sound a hundred times better than he could ever have imagined. He cut her off, the words spilling out. "Even if I want to, I won't always be able to tell you everything, Adria. But what you can always expect and get from me is the truth. I don't know who leaked to the *Post* that there was more to this investigation. I don't know what was intimated. But I won't file my report until I have all the answers."

Adria felt his intensity like a living force. It took several moments for his actual words to sink in. To have someone like Dane, a man with such drive and determination, on her side . . .

No, she corrected herself. Not on *her* side. Dane was on the side of truth. Which was as good. Better maybe. Because Adria was speaking the truth. She had not been negligent.

If he was as good as he claimed, and looking at him right now she would even guess he might have understated his abilities, then he'd find proof of that third plane.

Adria fought down a sudden smile. He had made it clear on more than one occasion what he thought of her side of the story. But that hadn't kept him from getting swept up in it.

He'd seized on it. He covered it well, but beneath that controlled exterior, Adria would bet her life—and likely was—that his mental wheels were spinning even faster than hers had. All the questions and inconsistencies were being played and replayed, analyzed and dissected, as he looked for that final pattern, where all the pieces fit, where the answer was incontrovertible. Where the answer was fact. And for her, proof.

And she was just as certain that he was fighting the process tooth and nail. Why? Because it went against his logical mind to believe in something so farfetched?

Or was it because of her? Was it personal?

The undercurrents zinging around his office hadn't escaped her. She'd fought recognizing the interest in his eyes, the probing looks, the open calculation of what she was really all about. The idea that he'd actively focused his powerful interest not only on solving her case, but on herself as a woman, shook her more deeply than she wanted to admit. Or deal with. Not now.

She looked at him. Animated, intense, alert. And attuned to her.

She'd roused the predator.

Great. Now what in the hell was she going to do with him?

Get him to keep her job, that's what. And that's all.

"I appreciate your dedication." She finally did smile when he frowned. "And I'll hold you to your promise. If you don't file your report until you get all the answers, then I know I'll be proven innocent."

THREE

Adria answered her phone two days later, crossing her fingers that it was Pete. She'd left three messages on his machine, none of which he'd answered.

"Ms. Adria Burke?" It wasn't Pete. It was a woman.

"Yes?"

"I'm a reporter. I'd like to ask you a few questions about the incident that occurred over Metro Airport last Monday."

"No." The answer had been immediate, instinctive. Had someone finally put two and two together? Had the mysterious "inside source" divulged the existence of the third plane? "I have no comment to make on the current investigation."

"So, you're saying there is an ongoing investigation?" the woman asked, her tone polite, yet entreating. It was that "trust me" voice Adria was convinced all reporters were taught the first day of journalism school.

"I'm not saying anything," Adria replied in the same tone. "However, I'd like to ask you a question."

There was a pause while the woman obviously weighed the value of taking the bait. "Go ahead," she said finally.

Adria tightened her grip on the phone. Dane had shown her the article before she'd left his office that evening. She squeezed her eyes shut trying to remember the byline. Sarah. "Is this Sarah Greene? Are you the reporter responsible for the story in the *Post* several days ago?"

"Yes, I am," came the quick, assured, response.

So, she was confident. Because of her source? Adria was dying to find out who it was and how much information this person was privy to, but she knew better than to ask straight out. "I'm sure you know that until the standard investigation is concluded, all involved are encouraged not to discuss the matter. Well, obviously you got someone to bend the rules a bit and discuss this with you. I have to admit to being curious as to who this person is."

"I don't reveal sources, Ms. Burke, if that is what you're getting at."

"What I'm getting at is you wouldn't be calling me unless you thought there was something going on here. As far as I know, this is just a standard review." That was a lie, but one she told without compunction. This reporter would likely sell her down the river for a story, so Adria figured she might as well steer the boat as long as she could. "But if it's more than that, my job could be at stake. Now, frankly, I'm not all too concerned about the outcome of the investigation with the facts as I know them." Another lie, but she held an even tone. "So if you've uncovered something that may change that fact, then I'd like to know what it is. I don't care who told you, just what was said."

The pause this time was almost nonexistent. "You're saying that if I pass along the information my source is giving me regarding the case, you'll talk to me about what you know?"

"I'm saying that if there is something else going on here that I don't know about that could adversely affect my career, then my loyalties may alter." Oh, how her ex-husband would love this, she thought disgustedly. Make them believe they were getting something while promising nothing. Serve only your best interests and everyone else be damned. She thought she might be sick.

"I'd have to have something more concrete

than that to go on before I told you anything," the reporter replied carefully.

Adria expected nothing less. But she wasn't just going to hand out information. All she had to do was figure out what she could give the woman without jeopardizing her situation or Dane's investigation. She didn't want to risk tipping anyone off about the third plane while Dane was still actively trying to find proof of its existence.

"Why don't we meet?" Adria suggested. "I'd feel better about this if we were face-to-face." It took some further convincing, but when the woman realized it was the only way Adria would talk, she finally agreed.

"There's a playground on Stratford, do you know it?" Adria asked, thinking quickly, figuring no one there would pay attention to two women chatting in the shade.

It wasn't until she'd given directions and hung up that she realized how easily—naturally—she'd thought of Dane as her partner in this, not as an adversary.

The idea alarmed her more than it reassured her.

Now the question was, should she tell him about this meeting before? Or after? Her first instinct was to wait until after. That way she could defuse his anger—and she had no doubt he'd be angry, whether he let it show or not—with whatever information she was able to get.

But her second instinct told her that her rationale was just a cover for fear.

She scooped up the phone and punched in Dane's number.

She'd stopped playing the coward five years ago. She'd managed to handle the Predator so far, she wasn't about to give away her edge now.

What in the hell was he doing hiding behind an overgrown jungle gym? Dane still hadn't quite figured out how Adria had conned him into this. One minute he'd been arguing with his superior, Roy Forster, who was riding him harder than usual to get his preliminary report in, the next he'd been sideswiped by a very feminine, very excited voice on the other line, explaining why he had to come to a meeting she'd set up with a reporter. At a playground, of all places.

Dane pulled at his shirt collar as sweat mixed with the heavy starch, making his skin itch. It was blazing hot out here. He'd given up trying to blend in thirty minutes ago. He was certain at least two mothers already thought he was some sort of pervert and wouldn't be surprised if several more were contacting the authorities on the portable phones in their minivans as they drove home.

He pulled a handkerchief out of his breast

pocket and wiped his forehead. He tortured himself with images of his air-conditioned office and an ice-cold can of Coke. He was missing lunch for this. Not that the cellophane-wrapped sandwich he'd have likely bought from the vending machine was a great loss.

Dane peered through the wooden slats of the jungle gym. They were still talking. What had Adria gotten herself into? And why was he standing here letting her get into it? She could be destroying the whole investigation.

She wasn't stupid, far from it, but he wouldn't put it past the reporter to somehow get her to slip up. He groaned, picturing the headlines if that third-plane scenario leaked out. His boss would have his ass in a sling by nightfall if Adria's story ever hit the papers.

Tension tightening the base of his scalp, he looked away, just in time to glare at a small boy who had been ready to drop a fistful of gravel on top of his head. The boy hurried on to some other unsuspecting target.

Dane couldn't recall ever being with so many kids at one time. Children weren't something he thought about often, if ever. His thoughts turned to his sister Dara and Zach. He wondered if they planned on having a family. It was a subject he'd never talked about. Not with Dara, Jarrett, or Zach. Why did that seem so strange now?

His lips twitching a little, he watched a mom whoosh down a slide with a giggling toddler trapped between her thighs. Dara was great with kids, her job a testimony to that. And Zach would make a good father. If Dara ever let him actually hold one. Zach's job as owner of an outfitting service that catered to thrill seekers would have Dara gray long before her time, he was sure. But their kids would be in heaven.

The image of several towheaded kids romping around Zach's big country house played through his mind. He felt . . . he wasn't sure. Melancholy. He frowned, then purposely shook off the whole disturbing thing and looked down at his watch.

Adria's time was up. He didn't care what she said, he was taking over. And no matter what, that reporter wouldn't be leaving here with any information.

He stepped out from behind the wooden tower. The table Adria and the reporter had been sitting at was empty. "What . . . ?"

"Looking for me?"

He swung around to find Adria standing in front of him. She looked remarkably cool in her lemon-colored blouse and pleated khaki shorts. Her fresh-as-a-daisy appeal only darkened his mood.

"I thought we agreed you trusted me to handle this." The disappointment he felt shouldn't be personal. But it was. "What in the hell are you doing talking to a reporter?"

If Adria was surprised by his outburst, she didn't show it. She took his arm and pulled him away from the play area. "Watch your language," she admonished.

Dane grunted, shocked at how close to the surface his emotions were. He didn't examine too closely exactly what those emotions were. "I'm sure these little monsters could teach me words I've never heard before."

She dropped his arm, and smiled at him. "My, my, a bit grouchy, are we?"

"I'm hot, I'm hungry, and I should be at my office getting some real work done." He glared at her. "I'm not grouchy."

She laughed.

It was an amazing thing. Her laugh. All light and airy. Her lips opened wide to reveal pretty white teeth. There was even a freckle or two on her nose.

She looked as if she belonged here, at this playground. With kids. Her own kids.

He didn't. He was a "tin-kicker." A man who spent too much time sorting through twisted metal looking for the cause of horrific devastation. Never had he imagined himself having a family of his own.

That he was now, with her, didn't scare him as much as it should have.

"Did you find out anything?" he asked as

they stepped onto the gravel parking lot. He was determined to stick to the matter at hand.

"Not much. Mostly I figured out what she doesn't know. Which is a lot."

"What did you have to give up to find out she knows nothing?" His tone was sarcastic. He doubled his effort at regaining his calm, detached perspective.

"I told her that I'd been reprimanded twice already and that I was a bit more worried than I had let on."

Dane went on full alert. This was something he hadn't questioned her about, as it didn't pertain to his specific investigation thus far. But there was no denying he was curious about why she'd taken two reprimands lying down. The Adria Burke he was coming to know didn't take anything lying down.

"Your work history is a matter of record for anyone wanting to find out," he said carefully. "She could have gotten that on her own."

Adria smiled. Only this time there was nothing light or airy about it. It was smug and confident. And sexy as hell. "Yeah, but she took it anyway."

He found himself leaning closer to her, even though he had no trouble hearing what she was saying over the shrieks of the children.

She stared up into his eyes, and the silence spun out between them. After what seemed like an eternity, she stepped away, the movement casual.

At that moment Dane was quite sure he could spend hours simply watching her move, talk, walk. Anything. Everything. With great determination, and not a little irritation, he again found himself having to force his mind back to the matter at hand. "And what's to keep her from blabbing that all over the papers? Surely she didn't just spill everything because you played the poor defenseless employee?"

All amusement fled her face, leaving it empty and austere. "I'm better at playing defenseless than you might imagine. I had years of practice."

Before he could even open his mouth, not that he knew what he'd have said, she went on. "She obviously knew I was the suspended controller when she called. You'll just have to trust me when I tell you I didn't give away anything. You'll also have to trust me that I don't think her source is from my end. Mark Beck is the only one, except you and the pilots, who knows about the third plane."

"And what makes you so sure it wasn't Beck who talked?"

She faced him squarely, her hands on her hips. "Because he's a walking, talking regulations manual. And because he's almost as much of a tight-ass as you are. Hard as that is to believe."

She stalked off toward a small turquoise-colored sedan, opened the door, and got in. Dane managed to get to her car before she pulled out. He rapped once on the roof and motioned for her to lower the window.

She resisted for a moment, then did as he asked, lowering all four windows. Heat rolled out in a wave over him, but it was nothing, Dane thought, compared with the heat that rolled through him whenever he was around her.

"Yes?" she said.

"We aren't done discussing this yet."

"No," she corrected him calmly. "*You* aren't done discussing this. Frankly, I've had about all the subterfuge, interrogation, and doubt I'm willing to take for one day. If you want to talk about this any further, call me when you think you're up to doing it without all the attitude."

She started to roll her window up, but Dane placed his hand over the edge. He was almost certain he was about to have his fingers smashed, but he stubbornly held on. In the end, she finally relented.

His jaw tightly clenched, he leaned down and brought his face level with hers. "I'm not doubting your word. It's just that I never take anything at face value. It's what makes me good at what I do." It was a fact, not a boast. "If you want to make sure you keep your job, then you have to work with me. And when you work with me, you play it my way. When I want your help, I'll ask for it. No more meetings with reporters." She opened her mouth, but he leaned a bit closer. "And no more running away the minute things get tough."

She didn't appear the least offended, or intimidated, though he'd used his very best—and always effective—"take no prisoners" tone.

"Yeah, well, that was always my problem, Colbourne."

"What? Running?"

"No. Staying through the tough part and only realizing afterward that I should have run."

Dane watched in silence as she drove away.

FOUR

Dane let his finger fall away from the doorbell, deciding a sharp knock would be better. His uncustomary hesitation had him pounding more forcefully than necessary on her door.

He'd managed to go almost forty-eight hours without giving in to his need to see her again. Of course, this visit was entirely business-related. Just as the reprieve had been necessary so that he could examine and analyze additional information before confronting her again. So what if this was a bit outside usual investigation protocol? With Adria Burke, outside of protocol was fast becoming standard operating procedure. A good investigator was flexible.

So why did it feel that by coming here—coming to her—he'd lost a battle?

And he never kidded himself. He was a sore loser.

The door swung open just as he was getting ready to pound on it again.

Adria, dressed in white denim cutoffs and what had to be the world's oldest Redskins jersey, ducked quickly, then straightened. "Why do I get the feeling you wish my reflexes were slower?"

Before he could respond, or apologize for almost smashing her nose, she stepped back and waved him inside.

"Actually," she said, closing the door behind him. "I'm glad you're here. I was planning to call you today anyway."

I'm glad you're here? After that scene in the playground parking lot, Dane had expected *her* to be the one to come out swinging.

He followed her inside, purposely keeping his eyes on her back. There was no protocol that covered what to do with legs like hers. He decided he could easily fill a manual on the subject.

Grateful for the distraction of the decor in the living room, he moved to the mantel that framed a small stone fireplace to examine the wing prop displayed there. It was an original, beautifully handcrafted out of wood, the surface hand-oiled.

"Remarkable workmanship."

"My grandfather's," she responded. "The

prop I mean, not the workmanship. It's from his first private plane, a—"

"Piper Cub," Dane broke in. "Nineteen thirty-nine or about, right?"

She smiled. "Right."

Dane examined it more closely. "Progress is a great thing, but you just don't see craftsmanship like this anymore."

Adria moved to his side. "I know. It's almost like art."

"Is that why you have it? In that condition I imagine it's worth a penny or two."

"If you mean do I get aesthetic pleasure from looking at it, then the answer is yes, I do. But I own it because it is a piece of my heritage. I could care less what it's worth on the open market. I would never sell it."

Dane didn't doubt her passion for her family, like her passion for aviation, was honest and strong.

He thought of his own father. Of the plane crash that had taken his life. For the first time he desperately wished he had a piece of that plane. One more mangled piece of history to add to his heap, he told himself, trying to ignore the hollow feeling inside his chest.

He moved to the end of the mantel and picked up a square piece of wood on which another blade had been mounted. This one was about six inches tall and polished to a shiny silver. There was a rather wicked prong sticking out from the side.

"That's a propeller fin," she said.

"From inside the compressor section of a jet engine. I have one very similar to it. Of course, mine's a little worse for the wear. It was one of the few recognizable pieces left after a crash I investigated about five years ago. And even then it took some imagination to figure out what it was."

Dane kicked himself for saying anything. Why had he opened himself that way? And if what he did for a living repulsed her, why should he care? But he did.

He turned to her to gauge her reaction. Plain to see, on her face, was simple understanding. She stepped closer and he saw more—interest, along with a healthy dose of curiosity. And she was making no effort to hide any of it.

She nodded to the propeller blade. "That was actually an award given to my father after he averted what could have been a major air disaster. He saved it from going to your collection, I guess." She smiled. "I'll show you the rest of mine, if you show me yours."

Something hot and heavy punched him low in the gut. Right at that moment Dane couldn't think of one thing he'd like better than to play show-and-tell with Adria Burke.

Again, he'd been in her presence for all of

five minutes and he'd lost his professional edge. If he'd ever truly had one around her. He cleared his throat as he set the fin down and stepped away. "Perhaps some other time," he said, hating the stiffness of his tone, even though he'd intended it.

Her smile faded, but the curiosity in her gaze remained. He didn't think she was still thinking about their respective collections either.

Dane fought the urge to fidget with his tie. He never fidgeted.

"Would you like something to drink? Iced tea?"

"Coke," they said simultaneously. She laughed.

Dane wanted to groan. "That would be fine. Thanks."

He sat on the couch and straightened his tie. Twice.

Adria pulled two glasses down from the cabinet and held one of them against her forehead. The man had presence all right. She'd spent time with him in two small, airless rooms and held her own. Now she was in a big, airy house—*her* house—and he seemed more imposing than ever.

"I'll show you mine if you show me

yours," she muttered under her breath. What in the hell had she been thinking?

She knew what *he'd* been thinking. And she found herself not minding it all that much. In fact—

Adria quickly filled the glasses with ice and Coke, took a deep, steadying breath. Think about how you're going to explain last night's phone call, she ordered herself, and not the fact that the four-poster bed you've pictured him looming over—naked—is right upstairs. She groaned. Not picturing Dane Colbourne naked. Talk about mission impossible.

"Here we go," she said a bit too brightly as she entered the small living room.

He stood and took the glass she extended to him. "Thanks."

They both sat down, he on the couch, she several feet away on a bentwood rocker. Any safety she'd felt with the small distance evaporated when he pinned her with that gaze of his.

"What did you want to see me about?" she asked quickly, deciding to let him go first. "Did you find out anything on who's talking to the *Post*?"

Dane shook his head. "Nothing on that."

"Anything on the third plane?" She hated the obvious thread of hope in her voice, but it couldn't be helped.

Again, Dane shook his head.

Frustration snapped and unraveled inside her like old elastic. Adria bounced up and immediately began pacing. "But the primary *was* there. It had to be on the tapes." She was talking to herself more than to Dane. She'd barely slept since the incident.

She turned again to Dane. "Is there *any* way the tapes could have been tampered with?"

He stared at her with something that remotely resembled disappointment. So she turned and paced back to the fireplace rather than look at him.

"Whatever tangible evidence there is on this case, we'll find it, Adria."

She whirled on him. "You keep saying that, but I'm not seeing any of it!"

Dane stood and closed the distance between them. "That's because there's damn little out there to be found."

"Then keep looking." She ducked around him, crossed back to the couch, and sat. A sip of her drink cooled her a little.

Dane sat down next to her. "I'm getting some additional pressure to turn in my preliminary findings. And I have to tell you, what I have right now doesn't make you look too good."

Determination surged through her, helping her hold on to what was left of her control. "Maybe I can give you something."

His gaze narrowed dangerously. "Maybe you what?"

"I got a phone call at three o'clock this morning. A warning."

"Whoa, back up." He pulled a pen and notepad from his inner jacket pocket. "Do you know who it was?"

Adria stifled a sigh. God forbid she just tell him anything straight out. It had to be at his command. "No," she said evenly. Her tense expression daring him to interrupt, she continued. "The person whispered, so I can't be sure if it was someone I know or not. I couldn't even tell the gender."

"What exactly did they say? Word for word."

"Don't talk to the press again."

"That's it? Don't talk to the press again?" He snapped the notebook shut and slipped it back inside his jacket.

Repeating the caller's words out loud made them seem even more real. Ominous. But obviously he didn't share her concern.

"Isn't it enough? Someone is threatening me, for goodness' sake."

"Did they say that?" he asked, clearly unimpressed.

"Well, no, but it *is* implied."

"Implied? Not really," he said. "Not that that will carry any weight."

"Well, it did with me!" She'd never match

him in calm demeanor, so why bother pretending? "I don't know about you, but being woken up in the middle of the night by a menacing voice on the phone isn't my idea of no big deal. Someone knows I talked to Sarah Greene."

He didn't say anything for several beats. There were times when his unruffled manner infuriated her. Okay, most of the time *he* infuriated her. She purposely crossed her legs and her arms, letting body language do her talking.

Dane downed the rest of his drink and remained silent a few moments more. "Okay, I'll see what I can turn up."

"Thank you," she said, a shade too dryly. She loosened her arms, resting her elbows on the arms of the chair. He seemed to relax a bit as well. It was hard to tell.

"There is a reason why I stopped by," he said.

Adria kept her casual position, but something in his tone made her want to hug her arms close again. This time for comfort. "Why do I get the feeling I'm going to like this about as much as getting crank calls at three A.M.?"

"The two planes involved"—he shot her a warning look when she opened her mouth to correct him, then went on—"have been examined. Both are missing some pieces of fuselage. Right now we're determining the ground area where they're most likely to turn up."

Adria quickly put together the importance of this information. "If you find anything that's not a part of either plane, then that will substantiate my theory." She tried not to let the excitement build inside her, but it was good news badly needed. Her emotions had been on the worst sort of roller-coaster ride, one she didn't seem able to get off. "How long will it take?"

"It's a very broad area, some of it forested. It may take some time to cover it all. And they may not find anything at all," he warned. "It happens sometimes. I wouldn't get my hopes up too high."

"It's my whole life we're talking about here," she said quietly. "I *have* to hope."

Dane nodded. "Even if they do find something, it might not prove conclusively that a third plane was involved. In which case, we're right back to where we started."

"Not exactly," she countered. "Someone thinks there is something important enough about this investigation that the idea of me talking to the press is making them nervous. I'm not playing Tom Clancy here, Dane. But I honestly believe that the third plane is somehow tied up with the phone call."

Whatever Dane thought of her theory

wasn't readable in his expression. No surprise there.

"I'll let you know if the search teams find anything," was all he said. He stood and headed to the foyer.

Adria stood as well, surprised to find herself wishing he'd stay. But she'd exposed her emotions and vulnerability to him more than enough for one day. Besides, wasn't handling stuff like this all part of the independence she wanted so badly?

He suddenly turned around, causing Adria to skid to keep from walking right up into his chest. She hadn't realized she'd been practically running after him.

"If you get any more phone calls, get in touch with me right away." He pulled a card out of his infamous inner pocket and jotted a number on the back, then handed it to her. "My home number."

She stared down at the neat, precise writing. So legible it could have been typewritten. Figured. "You should have been a doctor."

Confusion creased his forehead.

"Your handwriting. Nurses and pharmacists across the country would revere you."

He looked a little nonplussed, but said, "Thanks. I think." The corners of his mouth kicked up slightly.

God help her if he ever actually smiled. "I, uh, no problem." Oh great, now she was stuttering. She leaned forward to open the door, hoping he didn't see the heat she felt in her cheeks.

She didn't move back quite fast enough and Dane's chest brushed along her arm and breast as he moved past her. Now heat was a problem in more body parts than she could hide. She took a step back, hoping he'd leave quickly.

Dane was halfway out when he turned again, forcing Adria to face him. She wanted to groan. What was it about this man? Go. Stay. Both words were on the tip of her tongue.

"If there is more to this, I'll find it. Trust me on that."

She realized she did. Not just because she was strongly attracted to him. Or because she had no one else to trust. But because of his decency. Granted, it was well hidden most of the time behind his autocratic attitude, but bottom line—Dane Colbourne was a decent man.

She just hoped he was as good an investigator as he kept insisting he was. It was becoming alarmingly apparent he'd have to be if she had a prayer of coming out of this mess with her career intact.

"Thank you. Will you call me when you find out anything?"

He gave her the sort of stare that made her

supremely self-conscious. The sort of stare that made her *really* wish she wasn't wearing raggedy shorts.

If she was as candid as she liked to think she was these days, she'd admit it was the sort of stare that made her wish she wasn't wearing anything at all.

She felt herself lean toward him as if drawn into his heat. He lifted his hand toward her face, then just as suddenly dropped it.

"I'll be in touch, Adria," he said, his voice darker and a bit rough. This time he walked away without looking back.

Adria. First "the look," then "the name." She watched him drive off, and only when he was completely out of sight did she give in to the need to fan herself. And it had nothing to do with the August sun.

FIVE

Dane jerked his head off his desk when the phone beside his ear leaped to life and threatened to deafen him. A quick glance at the clock showed it was two-thirty in the morning. He'd been asleep for less than thirty minutes. He grabbed the receiver before the second ring, a sinking feeling telling him that those scant thirty minutes were all he was going to get. Please, he asked silently, let all the planes be in the sky where they belong.

"Colbourne."

"It's Adria Burke. I'm sorry to disturb you."

He bolted upright. Disturb him? You don't know the half of it, he thought morosely. Most of those thirty minutes he'd spent sleeping had featured Adria as the star player in erotic dreams. "What's wrong? Did you get another call?"

"Yes. Just now."

"Same person?"

"I couldn't tell. I think so."

"Same message?"

"No."

She sounded anxious, but not hysterical. Still, that she didn't immediately burst into a full explanation spoke volumes to him. She was spooked.

"I'm glad you called." He hoped she didn't read the depth of sincerity there was in those words. "Will you be able to go back to sleep?"

A moment's hesitation, then: "Probably not."

He held back the question her response immediately prompted him to ask. His restraint lasted about five seconds. "You want to talk?" Her long sigh told Dane he'd done the right thing. The pleasure that gave him made him wonder if it might also be his biggest mistake. "You got any Coke?"

If a smile could be heard, he heard hers. "I think I can manage that," she said.

Dane instantly felt revved up to full speed. "I'll be there in less than an hour."

"Thank you, Dane."

Damn, did she have to say his name like that? All soft and breathy? It had been a long time since he'd heard anything that sounded half as good as Adria Burke's voice at two-thirty in the morning. Dane gripped the phone tighter. "No problem." He worked hard for nonchalance. "I'm up, you're up. We might as well go over it now. If the phone rings before I get there, let the machine get it. Understand?"

"Yes, sir."

Even tired and unsettled, she didn't let up on him. "I like 'Dane' better," he said before he thought better of it.

This time he hung up first.

Adria met him at the door with a huge glass, filled almost to the rim with ice and Coke.

"Thank you," he said. She smiled lightly and traded the glass for his briefcase.

"Come on in."

He followed her down the hall, nursing the Coke, taking in her clothes. He couldn't say which was worse—the ragged cutoffs she had on last time or the gray sweats she now wore and that clung to her legs. Her shirt wasn't as old as the Redskins jersey, but she'd tucked it in, revealing the shape of her backside.

She's been harassed by some weirdo on the phone, he reminded himself. *The last thing she needs is you drooling over her.*

They entered the kitchen and Dane

glanced around. No plane parts in here. The room was average size, with standard appliances in standard colors. But it was warm, homey somehow. Maybe it was the woman occupying it that made it seem that way.

The center of attention was a large oak pedestal table flanked by four ladder-back chairs. Adria put his briefcase on the table, sat down on the other side, and snagged her cup of coffee.

"Please." She nodded at the chair in front of him.

He started to slide the briefcase to the floor, then changed his mind. It might be wiser to keep the constant reminder in sight. He swallowed more of his Coke and allowed himself another glance at her. Her hair was pulled back in a loose ponytail and her face was pale. There were shadows under her eyes that hadn't been there before. It was probably the lighting. He really wanted it to be the lighting.

The thought of her being terrorized by strange phone calls in the middle of the night had his stomach muscles tightening. One call he could dismiss—and he'd done a lousy job of that—but two calls . . .

The instincts riding him now were unfamiliar. They were primal, basic. The sort that made men go out and confront dragons. Because there was simply no other alternative.

Dane shook off the rather intense, unsettling feeling as he clicked open his briefcase and took out a pen and notepad. He felt ridiculously obvious in his attempts to armor himself, but she didn't appear to notice. Besides which, no matter how much he might wish it, she wasn't the dragon he wanted to fight. It would be so much easier if that were the case. Instead, she was rapidly becoming the damsel he wanted to fight the dragons to win.

"I appreciate your coming over," she said quietly.

He shrugged and began flipping the pages, looking for a clean one. "Like I said, I was up, you were up."

Out of the corner of his eye, Dane noticed Adria's gaze stray to his shirt. She'd done that at the door, but he hadn't paid much attention then. Now he looked down at the dark blue polo shirt, but didn't see anything strange. His eyebrows rose in question.

"Sorry," she said, color blooming in her face. "It's just I've never seen you without a suit on."

Heat crept into his own cheeks. He didn't know why he even bothered trying to keep things businesslike with her. He damn well knew he didn't want to. "Did you think I slept in a suit, too?"

Her widening eyes told him he'd missed dry humor by a mile.

"You weren't in—I mean, when I called, you were working." She stumbled over her words. "You *were* at your office."

"Yes, I was." He'd been at work all right, but she *had* caught him dreaming. His thoughts tumbled from falling asleep at his desk way too often to not wearing suits, to wondering what it would be like to fall asleep not wearing anything and being with her when he did it.

It was a powerful image.

He shifted in his seat and took another sip of Coke. It was icy cold but did next to nothing to cool him down.

"The phone call," he finally said. "You want to tell me about it?"

Adria studied her coffee as if she expected wisdom to rise with the steam and penetrate the fog in her brain. What was wrong with her? She was thirty-one years old, married and divorced. Certainly well past the age of stuttering and blushing around men.

But it was no wonder he had her all tongue-tied. A man who was only interested in business had no business giving a woman "the look." He was too in control of every facet of himself not to know what he was doing. Or what effect it had on her.

She wanted to groan in embarrassment. Did he know what she was thinking? Dear Lord. Tony had taunted her too often with her inability to mask her thoughts for her not to be aware of that particular shortcoming. It was still on the long list of things she was trying to change.

Dane's chair scraped the floor, startling her. He'd shifted closer.

"When did the call come in?"

It wasn't until she exhaled that she realized she'd been holding her breath. "Two-thirty. I called you right after."

"And the first call? That came at three?"

Adria silently thanked him for keeping his attention on the notes he was making. "Yes. It was the same whisper. I think it was the same person."

"What was the message this time?"

She swallowed the fear that knotted in her throat. " 'Keep talking and you'll lose more than your job,' " she quoted, not entirely able to keep her voice steady.

"That's it?"

"Isn't that enough?" she shot back.

"I didn't mean to imply it wasn't," he said, his manner offhand, as if he didn't really care one way or the other that she'd been scared out of her wits. He was just an investigator doing his job.

A fact, Adria instructed herself with brutal candor, she'd better get real straight, real fast.

Even if he was being "just an investigator"

alone with her in her small kitchen, at three-thirty in the morning.

"I haven't spoken to Ms. Greene again," Adria said, "or anyone else from the media. The only person I've talked to is you."

"Do you want to call the police?"

The question took her off guard. What, exactly, had she expected? That Dane was going to protect her from this unseen menace? The answer was painful to admit. That was exactly what she'd been thinking, albeit subconsciously, when she'd called him.

Stupid move, Adria, she admonished herself silently. Haven't you learned your lesson by now? She'd better hope so. Teachers didn't come any better than Tony Harris.

"I wasn't sure if notifying them was a smart idea." She was glad that this time at least she'd managed to sound calm and in control. Truth was, with some nut out there threatening her, and the Predator sitting at her kitchen table, she felt anything but calm or in control.

"It's up to you," he responded. "They can put a tracer on your phone, try to find out where the calls are coming from."

"And then what?" She went on without waiting for an answer: "I mean, you and I both know the chances of finding the person is small. It's too easy to call from a pay phone, or a cellular. And besides, I'm not completely sure this person isn't watching me. If my talking to you or Sarah Greene is making this person nervous, then I don't want to make a show of having the police trooping in and out of my house."

"But you called me. Let me come over here."

He was right. All that had mattered to her was that she'd heard his voice and felt safe. When he'd offered to come over, she hadn't wanted to say no.

"What makes you think you're being watched? Have you spotted someone? A car or anything?"

She shook her head. "No. It's just a . . . feeling." What she felt right now was foolish for saying anything. Her tone was a bit on the defensive when she added, "I don't know, I haven't seen anyone or anything strange around here. Certainly not at three in the morning," she added. "It's probably my imagination. But I don't know how else the caller could have known I'd talked to Sarah Greene or you."

"Unless the caller knows about Sarah's source." Dane was so alert the air around him fairly vibrated. "Or our caller is the source."

Our caller. It was amazing how reassuring that word was for her. But she and Dane weren't really a team, as much as she'd like to believe they were. He could still file a report claiming she'd been negligent.

"The only reason the source would threaten me is to protect his position as a paid informant. But frankly, I can't see where there's any real money in it. This isn't exactly Watergate."

"Okay. But that still leaves a caller who knows something we don't. Something he doesn't want anyone else to know. Something he thinks you already know and doesn't want to have spread around. To me, or anyone else."

"All I know," she said quietly, "is that there was a third plane. It was in exactly the right position to be involved in the collision. I can't think of anything else that someone would warn me about discussing."

Dane stiffened. "That third plane had to have had a pilot."

Adria's eyes widened. "Who would be solely responsible for almost killing several hundred people."

Dane swore under his breath. "Which makes you the perfect fall guy."

She nodded in understanding. "If the controller is proven negligent, no one would ever suspect the third pilot's culpability. Case closed. Question is," she went on, "why warn me? It just gives credibility to my story that there was something else going on in the sky that night."

Dane shook his head. "No, the question is: Who knows that you think something else is going on?" He smacked the table with his palm, making Adria jump. He didn't apologize. When he leaned forward, his eyes were almost glowing. "I've got to get my hands on that missing fuselage. If there was a third plane involved, he had two wings clipped. There has to be some evidence of that on the ground."

Adria gripped her cup so hard she thought it might crack. She peeled her hands off it and forced them into her lap. *He believed her.* Or as close as she was likely to get from him without concrete evidence. She closed her eyes for a second, sending up a quick prayer that the missing fuselage would be found and this whole horrible mess would be over soon.

"Adria?"

Her eyes blinked open. How did he do that? Infuse such intensity into one tiny word? That the tiny word was her name just amplified the effect on her.

"Yes?"

"You need to get some rest. Why don't I get out of here? I'll call you as soon as anything is reported from the field." He clicked his briefcase shut and shoved his chair back.

No. Adria was half out of her chair, leaning over the table to stop him. "Wait."

He froze, his gaze fastened on where her hand was gripping his wrist. As if his attention to that area had thrown on a power switch, Adria was immediately aware of the feel of his skin and muscle under her fingers. Without intention, her fingertips exerted additional pressure. His pulse leaped under her touch.

The combination of feeling him hot and alive under her fingers and watching emotions spark just as hot and alive in his eyes made her tremble.

The silence spun out; her will to move was nonexistent. The air between them charged up so fast that when Dane began to slide his gaze slowly from her hand up along her arm, she half expected to see a trail of fire. By the time he lifted his eyes to hers, she was not only trembling, she was burning up.

In less than thirty seconds, she'd felt as if he'd scented her, hunted her down, and trapped her. With nothing more than the beat of his pulse and those electrifying eyes of his.

Which made no sense. She was holding him.

"What?" he asked finally.

The question jerked her back to sanity. She let go of his arm. But he was quicker. He flipped his hand over and captured her wrist, his grip not painful, but inescapable.

"What do you want, Adria?"

What do I want? "Ask me something easy," she said shakily.

Without letting her go, he set his briefcase down and walked around the table toward her. Adria was trying hard not to let her sudden inability to breathe be too obvious. He stepped closer. She swallowed hard.

He raised his free hand and tucked a wayward strand of hair behind her ear. At the same time his thumb made slow circles on the inside of the wrist. She felt terribly unnerved. And unbelievably aroused.

"Why are you shaking?" When she didn't answer, he said, "Not an easy question either?" He reached for another strand of hair, but this time he let it slide through his fingers. "It can't be that I'm frightening you. I don't think anything frightens you. Not truly."

That's where you're wrong, she wanted to say. But the words were stuck deep in her throat. That he might continue this slow, intoxicating interrogation frightened her. But far more frightening, was the thought that he might stop at any second and walk away.

He ran a fingertip across the tender skin beneath her eyes. "You're not sleeping enough."

Right now she would settle for breathing. She wanted him to let her go. And yet she was the one who'd asked him not to go.

What *did* she want from him? His help? Yes. His expertise as an investigator? Yes.

To touch his face as he was touching hers? Oh, yes.

"Adria." This time her name was half warning, half groan.

Her gaze had become instantly riveted to his lips when he spoke. To feel that mouth on her? Is that what she wanted?

God, yes.

"This isn't smart," he said, moving closer still. "I should be in my car, heading home." She gasped when his knees brushed her legs. "Right now."

"Yes," she said. "Right now."

He let his hand drift to her chin, tilting it up slightly. "It wouldn't help. I don't sleep either." He broke off, then went on, his voice nothing more than a rough whisper. "You torture me in my dreams, did you know that?"

She gasped, then a tiny moan escaped her lips. She pressed her knees tightly together as a curling knot of sweet pain clutched hard between her thighs.

"And then I lie awake all night wondering things." He looked at her mouth with hunger so clear. "What does your mouth taste like, Adria?"

She shook her head slightly.

"Is that, 'No, you don't know'? Or, 'No, don't find out'?" He rubbed his thumb over her lip. "I'm an investigator, Adria. That's what I do." He leaned down, his breath warmed her lips. "Investigate."

Just when she thought he'd end her agony and kiss her, he lifted his head slightly.

The tiniest of twinkles flickered in his eyes. "May I?"

"You'd better," she answered hoarsely.

He slid one hand to cup the side of her face as he pulled her wrist up and placed her palm on his chest. He held it there, letting his heartbeat pulse heavily against her fingertips.

He dropped a torturously light kiss on her lips. "Remember," he warned. "I'm very thorough."

"God, I hope so," she breathed. Then slid her hand up into his hair and pulled his head down to meet hers.

Dane let her take his mouth. The sweet pressure of her lips as she took control almost robbed him of what little was left of his. She angled his head to one side and entered his mouth with her tongue, the action so slow and sinuous he had to make a concentrated effort not to lower her to the table right then and there.

He settled for tugging her closer, sliding his hands around to her backside and cupping her tight up between his legs. She was sweet and so hot and he . . .

He was losing his mind, that's what he was doing.

Instincts honed over too many years of keeping his emotions locked away took over. He held her hips and pushed her away gently.

She looked up at him, her eyes all dreamy and clouded with desire. "You're right, you know," she said, her voice delectably hoarse.

He'd all but begged to kiss her, then had stopped her. He'd expected her to be hurt or angry or both. God knows *he* wanted to rant and scream. "About what?" he asked, wondering why he still expected to be able to second-guess her. He should know better.

"To stop this."

Dane curled his fingers into his palm against the need to pull her back into his arms. "Maybe so," he said. "But it doesn't mean I wanted to."

She took a half step away. "What we want isn't always good for us."

"Adria."

She'd started to turn away, but stopped when he said her name. She looked back at him, her eyebrows lifted in question, as if she didn't trust herself to speak.

That he sensed no regret in her relieved him. "That's the problem. It would be good. Damn good. And we both know it."

Dane watched as she banked the emotions that were always so clear in her expression.

From the moment he'd met her, he'd felt she was too open. It was dangerous to be read so easily. He could never have survived like that. How had she? But now, when she worked to hide her feelings, it perversely angered him.

He thought she was about to say something, but she just shook her head, then turned to the table and cleared their mugs.

Dane knew he should pick up his briefcase and get the hell out of her kitchen. Out of her house. Out of her personal life.

It was the only logical, rational thing to do considering she was under investigation. An investigation being run by him. And though he was beginning to believe something else might have happened in the sky that night, that didn't automatically clear her name. He'd make damn sure he followed every available path and lead he had to its conclusion, but there could be no allowances made, no room for bias. For, or against.

He should push his growing personal involvement aside for now, then follow up on it after the case was over. But what if the final facts in the case didn't clear her? Proved her negligent? Cost her her job?

He might lose any chance he might have had with her.

Logical. Rational.

He ran his investigations that way. His career had flourished conducted under that code.

Only now did Dane realize that not only had his cold, unemotional approach adversely affected his private life, it had completely taken over. Until there were no personal aspects to his life.

He looked at Adria as she stood in front of the sink rinsing the dishes. The way his body tightened instantly, the things just looking at her made him feel—there was nothing logical, rational, or unemotional about them.

And he had absolutely no desire to change that.

He shut down logic as he crossed the room, not stopping until he was right behind her. He turned her around, took her face in his hands, and then, just as deliberately, took her mouth with his.

He invaded her with his tongue, tasting all of her. He slanted her head and coaxed her tongue into his mouth until their kiss was no longer give or take but an equal sharing.

They were both breathing hard when he finally pulled his mouth from hers. He tugged her against his chest and was filled with an absurd need to pump his fist and shout when she willingly curved into him.

He realized then that he'd been wrong to assume the battle he waged had been with her. All along, it had been with himself.

"I know what your mouth tastes like now, Adria. And I know I want more." He acted on his words with another kiss—brief but drugging in its intensity.

"I don't seem to be able to do what's best for me for any length of time," she said. "But if you're not the best thing for me, then I'll console myself with the fact that you're probably going to be the best worst thing I've ever gotten myself into."

Dane's lips quirked. Adria reached up to place her forefingers on the corners of his mouth. She pushed. "But if I'm going to fall off the good-girl wagon, then you have to give too. I want to see you smile."

"I smile," he said in his defense, still rebelling against the idea that he'd become that rigid.

"Yeah, I can see that."

He bared his tightly clenched teeth. "How's that?" he asked.

"Oh, much better," she said with mock solemnity, then giggled.

At the delicious sound, he finally broke into a true grin. She choked, then gasped.

His smile disappeared. "What?" He'd been caught off guard by the depth of pleasure their teasing brought him. Now he suddenly felt horribly self-conscious.

"I was right," she whispered, more to herself than to him.

Feeling more awkward by the moment and really not liking it, he battled his curiosity.

And lost. "About what?" he asked warily, certain he was going to like her answer even less.

"Your smile. Oh my God, Dane," she said, "do you have any idea what it does to your face?"

Right now he was pretty damn sure his face was burning red. "No," he said.

"Good. Then do me a favor, okay?"

"Anything if it means we can stop this ridiculous conversation."

The trace of vulnerability that entered her blue eyes tugged at him. "Smile only for me." He was surprised by the almost shy request, but before he could comment, she pulled his head down close to hers and whispered heatedly, "And only when we're alone."

Her hoarse plea twisted the ache in his groin into an even tighter knot. It was as if she held his emotions on marionette strings and yanked them at will. But instead of angering him, it made him want to—

Dane slowly tested his grin out on her again.

Her response was a deep, appreciative sigh that ended on a soft moan. "Yeah, just like that."

He wondered who was getting more pleasure out of this, knowing it couldn't possibly be her. "Any other requests?"

"Yeah. Shut up and kiss me."

With pleasure, he thought, his lips already

on hers. She let her tongue slide languidly into his mouth. With *great* pleasure, he amended.

The trilling of his beeper startled both of them. He couldn't have said who moved more quickly out of the other's embrace. They'd both reacted like guilty schoolchildren caught kissing under the bleachers. It spoke volumes about how little a role reality had just played in their little interlude. It was obvious they'd both been a little carried away, that neither of them was prepared to deal with the consequences of getting involved.

Adria rushed back to the sink and began wiping down the basin and counter. Both of which were already spotless.

Cursing under his breath, he glared down at the number flashing on his pager. "Who the hell is calling me now?"

Adria stepped toward the door. "There's a phone on the wall over the counter."

"Where are you going?"

"I thought you might like some privacy."

What he would like was very private. And it had nothing to do with the phone. But all he told Adria was "Thank you."

She nodded and was gone.

Because he wanted to rip the phone from the wall and send it flying, he purposely lifted the receiver gently and punched each number with controlled precision.

Barely ten minutes had passed since he'd

given in to his personal wants, his own desires. Something he hadn't done since . . . Hell. He couldn't recall a single time.

He simply wasn't cut out for mixing personal with professional. But when he was with Adria, he couldn't keep the two separated.

Dane raked his hand through his hair as the phone on the other end rang repeatedly in his ear. "You'd better pick up," he said.

The ringing stopped as the call was answered. "Eliot."

"Colbourne."

"Good, glad I caught you," Eliot said. "You left instructions to be notified immediately if we got anything."

"And?" Adrenaline kicked in, the sweet rush bringing relief at being back in familiar territory.

"We got a call from some guy out in Indian Head about ten minutes ago. He's been out of town on business and came home early this morning to discover some fuselage in his front yard, caught up in some trees on his property. He called Metro and they connected him to us."

"I'll meet you out there." Dane made a mental note of the directions and hung up.

"Good news?"

Dane turned to find Adria in the doorway. His gut instinct was to play this one close to the vest. Too much had happened between them too quickly. The phone call was a much-needed wake-up call. It was time to step back a little.

Adria moved into the room. She must have sensed his withdrawal because she stopped beside the table. "That's okay, I understand," she said.

Dane had a sudden urge to tell her it was anything but okay. All he wanted to do was hold her and she stood there trying to be so reasonable.

"I have to go." He closed the distance between them, but only to grab his briefcase. He didn't dare take that last step to her. "You'll be okay?"

"Yeah."

"You could always check into a hotel for a while."

She shook her head. "No. I'm sure I'll be fine. It's almost morning anyway." She paused. "Thanks for coming over."

This was all wrong, he thought, even as his mind fought to regain its usual detachment. He managed a short nod, then left.

SIX

Dane wished he had grabbed some breakfast on the way to his office after another long night spent at the warehouse the fuselage pieces were stored in. Putting them together wasn't nearly as complex as putting together the jagged remains of an entire plane, but it had still been a challenging jigsaw puzzle. To his dismay, every last scrap they'd recovered belonged to either the Liberty or the AirWest planes.

Most of his time last week had been spent on computers, where, with the help of a team of other professionals, he had recreated the flight paths of the two planes. He had covered each aspect of the mishap, anything and everything that could disprove that the two planes had hit each other.

He didn't come up with one shred of

proof. All he had was a few crank phone calls and Adria's conviction that she was telling the truth.

He hadn't heard from her, so he assumed she hadn't gotten any more disturbing calls. But it had taken an enormous amount of discipline not to check up on that fact personally, telling himself that his time was better spent— for both of them—working on the facts of the case and letting Adria take care of herself.

His phone rang; another annoying sound adding to the pounding inside his skull. This time Dane welcomed the intrusion.

"Colbourne."

"How you coming with that report on the Metro mishap?" It was Forster, his boss.

Dane didn't mistake the command for a question. Forster had been an air-force colonel, but Dane wasn't sure anybody had told *him* that he was retired. Forster barked out orders and expected complete and swift obedience as if he was still in uniform.

Dane was half-surprised Forster didn't wear his silver eagle on his lapel.

"It's coming along," he said, knowing the vague answer was not what Forster wanted to hear. It certainly wasn't usual for Dane. Ambiguity was simply not characteristic of him.

"You've still got that Cairo incident on your desk as well as that mishap out in Seattle," he reminded Dane unnecessarily.

"I'm aware of that, sir. I've been putting time in on those as well." The only thing he hadn't put any time into lately was sleeping.

"I'd like to turn this one over to the FAA ASAP," Forster said. "So wrap it up."

"I still have a number of details to clear up before I can complete my report." Dane supposed it wasn't totally out of line to be getting pressure so soon. His preliminary report did make it appear as if the case would be open-and-shut. So why were his instincts clamoring?

"I want it on my desk before the week is out, Colbourne."

The sense of unease grew, but all he said was, "Yes, sir."

Dane hung up, then downed his entire Coke. "Time's running out, Adria," he muttered.

He stared at the open file in front of him, then at the stack of files sitting on the corner of his desk. "One more time," he told himself. Maybe this time he'd find something. The one clue he could take to this boss and use as a bargaining chip to continue the investigation.

Before he could reach for his pen, the phone rang again.

What now? He grabbed the receiver. "Colbourne."

"Dane?"

He immediately sat up straight. "Adria?" He realized instantly just how foolish he'd been to believe that distance and time had put his involvement with her back into the proper perspective. "What's wrong?"

"What makes you think something's wrong?" A bit sharply, she added, "I could just be calling to find out if any of the fuselage you found didn't match the AirWest or the Liberty."

"How did you find out about the fuselage?" Before she could answer, he said, "Never mind, I can guess. Our friendly reporter put another update in the paper." He'd been so absorbed in trying to uncover proof, he hadn't paid close attention to the media coverage.

It didn't take much to figure out that the man who'd found the parts on his lawn might have contacted the papers. "I'm surprised you didn't see it on the six o'clock news," he muttered.

"Actually, that's why I'm calling. There was a report on the eleven o'clock news last night from Indian Head, where the fuselage was found. I noticed something during the telecast that didn't seem right. It wasn't until this morning that it clicked. But I'm not sure I should say anything more over the phone."

Dane blew out an impatient breath. He wasn't sure why he was getting angry. Her motivation in calling was clearly professional, as it should be. So why was he mad and utterly disappointed?

"Listen," he said. "I've got a pile of folders on my desk, my boss breathing down my neck, and an open file that is begging to be shut. If you have anything concrete that can keep it open, tell me now."

Her tone turned to ice. "You're not the only one with problems, Dane Colbourne. You'll have to excuse me for thinking you wanted to find out the truth about what really happened up there that night. I'm telling you I have information. I don't want to discuss details over the phone. Do you want to talk to me or do I call Sarah Greene and take this up with her?"

"Don't talk to anyone but me," he said immediately.

"Don't order me around," she countered. "I'm calling you as an investigator, not because of what happened—" She broke off; he heard her take a breath. "Okay, bottom line. I'm attracted to you. We kissed. I, uh . . ." She faltered again. "You know I liked it."

Dane shifted on his seat. "You know I did too." The words out before he had decided to say them.

There was a pause, then she said, "You obviously haven't let that affect your investigation." Dane had to work harder than ever to keep from correcting her. He wanted it to be the truth as badly as she apparently did.

"And I agree it shouldn't," she went on.

"Name a time and place and I'll be there." He instantaneously realized it was the best and worst thing he could have done. Just don't let it be your house, he prayed. He'd run that gauntlet once; he knew better than to risk it again. "Anywhere but a playground," he added.

Adria leaned on the hood of her car and watched through the trees as the 727 lifted into the air; the roar as it went directly overhead vibrated her bones. It was as close to feeling like home as she'd felt in two weeks now.

A crunching sound signaled that a car had just pulled off the rarely used service road onto the gravel lot where she was parked. She saw Dane climbing out of a nondescript sedan that had government issue stamped all over it. He, and not the government, probably owned it.

Keep it light, she schooled herself. Cool. Professional.

Her fingertips pressed hard against the hood of her car. She didn't feel the least cool. And her thoughts as she watched him close the distance between them didn't even have a passing acquaintance with professional. An entire week's worth of tough decision making flew right out the window.

He looked good. The wind ruffled his hair, making her wonder what he'd look like in tight jeans and a body-hugging T-shirt. Not that his suit and starched white shirt didn't play up his beautiful face just as well.

That phone call had been hard enough. And she'd had only his deep voice to deal with. This might just kill her.

Reminding herself to keep it light, she asked, "Did you actually make payments on that thing?"

Dane's expression showed confusion, so she nodded to the car.

"So sporty and what a hot color. Gray." She smiled when he frowned. He was so easy to tease. *Watch it, Adria.* Even loose and light was getting her hormones into trouble. Cool and professional would have to do. Now, if she could only remember what that was.

"You don't exactly drive an Indy car yourself," he said in a flat voice, indicating her practical sedan.

"Yeah, but at least turquoise shows some style, some flash."

"I guess I'm not a stylish, flashy kind of guy."

Adria's smile faltered. She bit down hard on the words that almost escaped: What kind of guy are you, exactly? She didn't have to ask.

She already knew. He was obsessive about his job, a workaholic who was so involved in what he did for a living he didn't even have a clue about doing anything that could be construed as fun or relaxing.

And he was a guy who had made a science out of giving the perfect kiss. When had he found the time to learn that? she wondered.

Suddenly uncomfortable at the silence between them, Adria hopped off her car and reached inside the open passenger window. "I figured you hadn't eaten, so I sprang for lunch."

"That wasn't necessary."

"It's only fast food," she tossed back over her shoulder as she grabbed the white bags and drink tray. Carefully balancing her load, she turned to find Dane right behind her. As he took the drink tray from her she said, "Don't tell me you don't eat fast food. I figured you probably lived on the stuff."

His expression had gone from emotionless to strained. "Worse. Vending-machine food."

She made a face. "You're right, that is worse." The tension was almost palpable. If he didn't look so remote, so contained, she might have thought this was as difficult for him as it was for her.

Adria headed to the closer of the two picnic tables set up on the grass strip beyond the gravel lot. "I would have made something at home, but I figured if I was late, you'd leave."

He sat opposite her and started unloading bags.

Realizing she was babbling, but unable to stop in the face of his stony silence, she said, "It's all cheeseburgers, everyone eats those, and fries." She unwedged the largest of the two drinks and set it in front of Dane. "High octane, just the way you like it."

"Thanks," he said, still unsmiling, but made no move to eat.

Adria kept talking as she unwrapped and depickled her burger. "My dad used to bring me here all the time. We'd watch the planes take off and eat a picnic while he told me stories."

She looked up at Dane and realized she couldn't eat a bite. Not with him just sitting there and staring at her. Was his slip of control that night in her kitchen bothering him so badly? Did he expect some sort of statement from her that she didn't expect it to happen again? "Is something wrong?" she asked. "Aren't you hungry?"

Bad choice of words, she realized immediately. This time she was sure she heard him groan, even though he muffled it behind his tightly clenched jaw. And then he pinned her with "the look."

How did the man shift from impersonality to intimacy so swiftly? And thoroughly?

Adria tried not to squirm in her seat.

After several knee-quivering moments she finally tore her gaze away and scooped up her burger. She'd eat the whole thing even if she had to choke down each bite. The burger was halfway to her mouth when he spoke.

"I would have waited."

Her throat went dry. "What?"

"For you. I would have waited."

Adria couldn't say whose cheeks warmed first. They both looked away as the moment spun out and the air between them practically vibrated. If she hadn't been so unnerved, she would have laughed at the way they both simultaneously attacked their food like starving children.

Minutes later, the sounds of another take-off echoing distantly, Adria decided the safest—not to mention smartest—thing to do would be to get to business. "I was watching the eleven o'clock news the evening after you left," she began. She kept her eyes on her fries, drawing patterns in the ketchup she'd poured onto the burger wrapper. "They had a live remote from that guy's front yard. I noticed there were people roaming over his property. He seemed pretty isolated out there, so I knew it wasn't neighbors. I figured it was other media and maybe some of your guys still poking around."

"You figured right. I had men out there for three days. A lot of the fuselage was high up in the trees, so we brought in cherry pickers."

"It all looked normal, but something kept bothering me, something that wasn't right with this picture. Then I noticed Sarah Greene."

Dane seemed to tense a bit at the name, but all he said was, "That wouldn't be out of the ordinary. She was probably there to interview the man for a follow-up story in the *Post*."

"Exactly what I figured. But the feeling stayed anyway." She shrugged. "I didn't put it together until this morning when I got a phone call from her." Adria leaned forward, her fries forgotten. "It hit me the moment I heard her voice. She wasn't hanging back with the media types milling about, she was *behind* the taped-off area with the crew."

Dane shook his head. "You must be mistaken. No way would any of my team let an unauthorized person in to wander around an evidence site."

"Well, I hate to be the one to break this to you. But she was there."

Dane seemed to ignore this and asked, "What did she want when she called?"

"She asked if I'd heard anything more on

the investigation, asked if I knew when the report would be filed. She even hinted that she suspected I had an inside track."

This time Dane looked surprised. "What exactly did she say?"

"It wasn't what she said, more like how she said it. Intimating things." Adria shrugged. "I can't explain, but I got the distinct impression she suspected I knew more than I was letting on. Do you think she knows about us?" The minute the question left her lips Adria wished it back. His attitude made it more than clear there was no "us." She waited for him to point out that embarrassing fact.

He surprised her. "I can't see how," he answered, his tone completely matter-of-fact.

A little thrill shot through her. She knew she shouldn't, but being an "us" with this man would thrill any woman. She was only human.

"I hope you didn't let anything slip."

Well, maybe not *any* woman, she corrected silently as she glared at him. "Of course not. I told her the truth. I hadn't heard from anyone connected with the investigation in several days, since before the discovery of the fuselage." She narrowed her gaze. "I told her she probably knew more about that than I did."

"I didn't want to get your hopes up," he said, half under his breath.

Adria wasn't about to let him off that easily. "My hopes up? I'm a grown woman, Dane.

Don't go trying to protect me from the big bad world. Believe me, I've seen plenty of it."

Interest sparked in his eyes. "That's the second or third time you've said something like that," he said. He studied his french fries as if expecting them to perform some sort of trick. "I know this isn't any of my business, but—"

He's embarrassed, she thought. That he was clearly reticent about asking her to talk perversely made her want to tell him everything.

"I'm divorced," she said bluntly.

He looked up, and the interest she found there wasn't simply physical. It was personal. He didn't just *want* her, he wanted to *know* her.

"You probably have that in your file on me." A little nervous again, she took a steadying breath. "But what that file doesn't tell you is that my ex-husband, Tony Harris, was a controlling, manipulative man whom I allowed to run roughshod over me for six years."

"I can't imagine anyone controlling you."

Adria smiled. "Thank you. That's the nicest thing you've ever said to me." *Now I know what your mouth tastes like, Adria. And I want more.* "One of them anyway." Images of him kissing her again, putting his hands on her, his mouth on her—

"What made you finally leave him?"

"My job," she choked out. Clearing her throat, she went on. "Tony didn't mind my indulging my love of flying in long chats with my father and grandfather. But he drew the line at letting his wife actually fly herself."

"Do you?"

Pride swelled in her. Flying was the one thing outside of her job she'd made time for. "I do now. Soloed for the first time last year."

Dane's mouth kicked up the tiniest bit and Adria's heart skipped a beat at the threat. *Dear Lord, don't smile at me now.* "But that was just the beginning. Gramps died just before we were married, but I saw my dad often. He loved his job as a controller almost as much as he did flying. I was fascinated."

"I take it Tony didn't share your fascination."

"Not hardly. He was an attorney and proud of the fact that his wife didn't work."

There was a small, but distinct pause. "No kids?"

Adria shook her head. "Thank goodness."

Dane's eyes narrowed. "You don't want kids?"

Adria was intrigued by his response. From the way he'd acted at the playground, she'd expected wholehearted approval. "Not with Tony," she said, watching him more closely. But the mask slammed down again. "The way I tried to please everyone back then, if we'd had kids, I'm sure I'd have stayed with him out of some misguided rationale that the kids needed their father."

"Pleasing everyone gets to be exhausting," he said quietly.

"My mom passed away when I was young and I sort of took over taking care of Gramps and Dad."

"Who took care of you?"

His question caught her off guard, but before she could comment, he said, "They were lucky you were so strong. It's more than I was able to do." He looked faintly startled that he'd spoken.

"They loved me," she said. "And I loved them. They didn't force anything on me. It just happened. I didn't realize then the pattern it was establishing. At the time I'm sure they didn't either."

After a long while Dane spoke. "After my dad died, my mom and my sister sort of shut themselves off. Dad was our hero, but especially Dara's. She was like a miniature version of him." Dane's expression hardened. "I should have been there for them, but I had this big ball of anger inside me. There was a lot of speculation that my dad had been at fault. I was having a hard enough time dealing with him abandoning us. I was afraid if I stayed around too much, I'd eventually explode. I guess I knew that in a lot of ways, it was even worse for Mom and Dara. So I dealt with it by not being home any more than necessary."

Without quite realizing it, Adria reached out and laid her hand over his tightly clenched fists. "I'm sure you were all angry and hurting. There don't seem to be any rules when someone in your family dies. You just do what you think is best and work with the rest. I'm sure they all understood."

Dane lifted his fingers and trapped hers between them. "Thanks."

In that one word, she heard genuine gratitude, compassion, and a trace of relief. How long had he been carrying that guilt?

"I was the lucky one," he added. "I had two really great friends. We were the Three Musketeers of Madison County." His expression grew almost wistful. "They sort of picked up the pieces for me." He cleared his throat. "The investigators cleared my dad. I guess that was when I really began to work through my anger. I had a fact, a tangible thing I could look at and analyze."

Adria knew exactly what he meant. "Was that when you decided to become one yourself?"

He looked up, locking his gaze with hers. Adria drew in a short breath. She had a connection here with this man, she thought. As if he could see into her soul, and liked what he found. For the first time he'd opened that window, too. And she discovered she felt the same way.

"Probably the day the report came out," he answered finally.

"When my grandfather died," she began, needing to share with him as he had with her, "I was already engaged to Tony—"

"I can't imagine he was much help," Dane broke in.

"You're right, he wasn't. Actually, looking back on it, I think he was more relieved. I had been gently suggesting that he let me take flying lessons." She grimaced. "Let, allow. I can't believe how I used to think." She shook her head. "I eventually gave up on talking him into it. Instead I signed up to take my controller test."

"I bet that went over well."

"I didn't tell him, not until after I'd taken the test and passed. My dad helped me study. He was all for it. I don't know what I'd have done without him."

"How did Tony take it?"

"Saying 'not well' would be an understatement," she answered. "But going to Oklahoma City, to school, well . . . I guess he really didn't think I'd do it. He sure as hell worked on me and he knew what buttons to push. He had an incredible talent for making me feel selfish when I did anything for myself. He had a field day with this, pulling the 'poor me' act, saying he was hurt that he wasn't enough for me, that I needed more. Breaking free of that mentality was one of the hardest things I've ever done."

"Did you end it before or after you went to school?"

That he knew she, not Tony, had been the one to end it pleased her. "I signed up and he put his foot down. Frankly, I was surprised he didn't let me go more easily."

"He didn't want to let you go. He wanted someone he could control. If you left, how would he define himself?"

Adria was astonished by his insight.

"What made you finally do it? Where did you get the strength?"

"My father dying," she said plainly. "He had a heart attack. Too many cigarettes and not enough exercise—the bane of many a controller." Her gaze drifted back to their still-entwined fingers. She found strength there and, for the first time since her divorce, didn't feel afraid to take a little of it. "But it was losing his job during a strike that really killed him." Her eyes burned with unshed tears. "Just before he died, he apologized to me."

"For what?"

Adria wiped her eyes and sniffed. "I never complained about taking care of my dad and Gramps, but I won't deny that Tony's main appeal was his insistence in taking complete care of me. I willingly let him make all the decisions, control every facet of our lives. It was a relief. My dad understood that better than I'd realized.

"But the novelty wore off after a couple of years. Instead of feeling cosseted, I began to feel manipulated. But I learned very quickly that, for a lawyer, Tony was appallingly unwilling to compromise. Opposing lawyers were more successful at plea-bargaining with him than his own wife. My dad carried a lot of guilt because of that. I had no idea I'd let on how unhappy I was." She paused and Dane squeezed her hand. She smiled at him. "That's what he apologized for. And he made me promise that I'd do what *I* wanted. If Tony was the man he should have been, a man who really loved me, he'd understand, if not—" She shrugged. "Dad said I'd done enough for everyone else, it was time to do something for me."

"Sounds like a wise man. I wish I'd known him."

Adria smiled. "It would have been interesting, that's for sure."

Dane lifted a brow. "I'm letting you pour your heart out, being the understanding, sensitive guy, and you're insulting me?"

Heat filled her cheeks and she tried to tug her hand away. Dane tightened his grip.

"I give up," he said. "I've obviously been an investigator way too long."

Baffled, Adria asked, "Give up what?"

"Joking." He sounded so morose, she almost laughed.

"It's not the joke," she said seriously when she realized he was serious. "It's the delivery. If you didn't scowl, it would help."

"I don't—" He broke off and a moment later his expression turned sheepish. This time she did laugh. He scowled and she laughed harder. "Okay already," he grumbled. "Don't rub it in."

"I'm not. It's just that you're actually cute when you're embarrassed."

He opened his mouth, but shut it quickly. Heat climbed conspicuously into his cheeks. That just broke her up all over again.

Dane dropped her hand and circled the table threateningly. Giggling, Adria scooted off the bench and began backing away from him.

"Cute, huh?" he said, closing the distance between them with his long strides.

Adria's breath came in short gasps. The Predator was loose. And she loved it.

"Extremely," she taunted him. It was dangerous, she knew. But the thrill of it only spurred her on. "Not to mention sexy."

Her hips bumped up against another table and he stalked her, right up until he was standing between her legs.

She couldn't breathe at all now, much less speak. But talking was the last thing on her mind. And when he slid his palm around the back of her neck and dipped his head, his eyes told her it was the last thing on his as well.

SEVEN

The air reverberated with thunder, the table at her hips vibrated. Adria knew it was the effect of another jet roaring overhead, but as Dane subtly pressured her lips to open and slid his tongue inside, she knew she'd match his power to make her body vibrate against the thrusters of a jet any day.

Trailing openmouthed kisses to the sensitive spot just below her ear, he groaned deep in his throat. "You taste so good." He moved to her neck. "Remind me again why I'm not supposed to be doing this."

Adria slid her fingers into his hair as his tongue traced the line of her collarbone. She used her tongue to trace the shell of his ear.

"On second thought, don't," he ordered. His hands moved to her waist and he stepped closer between her legs.

Adria shifted her knees apart, welcoming his hard body against the ache that was tightening the muscles between her legs.

"Dane." Her voice was a harsh rasp. She sucked in her breath when he crowded even closer, moving his hips against hers. Warm air caressed her back and she realized he was pulling her shirt from her jeans.

I should be stopping him. His hand, warm and a little rough, smoothed across her lower back and up her spine. *But heaven help me, I'm not going to.* Dane swallowed her moan of pleasure, taking her mouth harder this time.

Adria gave right back. She gripped his hips, holding him tight against her, moving as he moved. Her fingers slid under his suit jacket and pulled at the cotton shirt.

He sucked in a harsh breath when her fingers brushed his bare skin. His skin was hot, smooth, and tightly wrapped around hard muscle. He felt better than Adria could possibly have imagined. And she wanted more.

But she was sidetracked from her mission when Dane shifted back, allowing his hands to move up between them. When he bent over her, Adria was forced to let go of him and brace her hands on the table behind her for support.

Her shirt was already bunched up. Dane merely nudged it higher then dipped his head and captured a distended nipple between his teeth before closing his lips tightly around it, pulling it with gentle rhythmic suction. His mouth felt wetter and hotter than anything she'd ever experienced. And that was through the fabric of her bra, a small barrier that was suddenly too much.

Dane lifted his head a fraction.

"Please, don't stop." The words were out before she could stop them.

He released the front catch on her bra, then lifted his gaze to hers. "I'm having a hard time not lifting you up on this table and crawling right up on top of you."

"Yes," she said hoarsely. Had she ever thought making love to Dane Colbourne would be something less than universe altering? She swallowed hard when he shifted against her. She rotated her hips right back.

With a sharp curse, Dane grabbed her hips and sat her down on the table. She wrapped her legs around his hips as he leaned her backward until her spine pressed against the time-worn wood.

He said something against her neck, then again as he trailed kisses down past her collarbone.

"Hmm?" Adria questioned, only distantly caring. His mouth felt perfect on her; her skin felt electrified.

"Splinters," he murmured. He left her only long enough to pull off his jacket and slide it beneath her. She immediately reached for his shirt, but he was faster. He bared her skin, pushing her shirt up and off, followed quickly by her bra. He laced his fingers with hers and pushed their hands overhead as he leaned over her again.

"Your shirt," she managed between gasps.

"What about it?" he said as his mouth trailed downward.

"I want it off."

With a predatory gleam in his eyes, he release her hands but not her gaze. Mesmerized, she watched as he slowly yanked off his tie, undid the cuffs, then the top two buttons of his shirt. He reached behind to grab the back of the collar and pulled the garment over his head. It joined his tie on the bench.

He was marble, from his shoulders and arms to a beautiful chest with just enough hair scattered across it, and a flat abdomen. Statues would be envious, she thought, licking her lips.

She reached up to caress him as he leaned over her. Hard as marble, maybe, but not cold. "You're so warm," she murmured, then gasped when his belly rubbed hers.

"Hot," he corrected her, then ran his tongue along her shoulder. "Burning up."

The combination of the warm sun and his wet tongue laving her nipple at the same time made her thighs tighten convulsively on his hips. She crossed her ankles behind his back and smoothed her hands up to grip his shoulders.

She bit down on a groan as he pulled one nipple into his mouth, but was unable to keep from crying out when he flicked his tongue over and around the engorged tip.

He immediately lifted his head. "Did I hurt you?"

She shook her head, beyond speech. She wove her fingers through his hair and pressed his head back to her breast. He understood.

His rhythmic sucking on one nipple, then the other, soon had Adria rocking her hips against his. He matched the motion, then intensified it, sending a thundering sensation through her.

Dane slid his hands to the waistband of her pants. "I should stop," he said without the least bit of conviction. "But I want to feel you all over me, Adria. God, but I don't think I've ever wanted so badly as I do now. What you do to me—" He broke off as she arched her back in response to his heated words, grinding her hips even more forcefully against his.

The rigid length of him rubbed against her, right where the ache was deepest. "I know," she panted. "I don't want you to stop, Dane. Not now."

His hands paused over the snap to her jeans, and trembled. She reached for the snap herself, willing to rip it out if it would get him inside her faster. Never, never, had she felt this frenzy. And yet, as wild and chaotic as her need for him had become, she was perfectly aware of exactly what they were about to do. And where.

And it just made it better.

He closed his hand over hers and completed the task. He pulled her pants and underwear down to her knees, then gazed at her hungrily. "A picnic table laid with a very tempting feast."

Adria sucked in her breath and held it there when he dipped his head. He slid his tongue slowly over the heated flesh between her legs. Only when he had her writhing beneath his mouth did he slip his tongue inside her. Over and over again he repeated the sweet torture until she was clutching at his hair as her inner muscles clenched tremulously with her release.

He kissed his way slowly up her abdomen, stopping at her breasts, which rose and fell sharply under his ministrations as she tried to regain her breath.

She dimly heard a buckle being undone, and a zipper. His hands felt big and warm when he gripped her hips. He slid his tongue to just beneath her ear. "Do you know I almost came when you did?" he said roughly.

She locked her legs around him and lifted

her hips in response. He was biting her chin when he drove inside her.

Adria moaned, long and low as he filled her again and again. His breath was coming in short grunts as he lifted away from her and slid her down—jacket and all—to the edge of the table. Hot tears of emotion slid from the corners of her eyes as she watched him hold her and thrust into her. There was a stark beauty in the way his hard body moved so gracefully, so perfectly against hers—into hers.

She felt him tighten inside her and watched in awe as the sun gilded him when he lifted his face to the sky and climaxed.

He looked back at her and held her gaze as the aftershocks rippled through him.

"You're beautiful," she whispered, finally giving voice to the words that had echoed in her head almost from the moment he'd entered her.

He looked down at himself, as if wondering what she possibly saw in him that would make her say that. She opened her mouth to convince him, but when he lifted his head, she forgot what she'd been about to say.

There was the sexiest smile curving his mouth. She wanted him all over again. And the need went far deeper than the physical.

"I'm standing here with my pants around my ankles, taking you like a rabid animal on a picnic table. That's beautiful?"

"No," she said. "It's perfect." Hell, she was close to shouting with the joy of it. "But I was referring to you. All of you."

"All of me? And here I thought you only liked me for my—what did you call it? My tight ass?" The sexy smile turned to a bad-boy grin she'd have never thought him capable of.

"That's playing dirty. No man should be allowed to carry a concealed weapon like that."

He laughed, the rusty sound the most wondrous thing she'd ever heard. "What, like a label on my zipper saying 'handle with caution'?"

She reached up and grabbed his forearms, yanking him off balance until he collapsed down onto her. They were nose to nose when he caught his weight on his hands. "Your ego is almost as big as your—"

He kissed her soundly, then said, "Are you complaining?"

She couldn't recall ever being this happy. "No. But the concealed weapon I was referring to was your smile."

Color crept into his cheeks. "And you blush real cute too," she added.

Dane gently bit her bottom lip. "Smartmouth," he said, then sucked her lip.

Just as Adria was contemplating whether or not he could possibly be ready to make love again so soon, he pulled her into his arms.

"Hold on," he ordered. She clamped her legs tightly around him as he lifted her, turned around, and sat down on the table, leaving her straddling his lap. When she tried to lean her head back, he cupped her head tightly to his chest. "No, not yet. Okay?"

"Perfectly," she answered. His heart beat a strong tattoo against her cheek, the rhythm exactly matching her own.

They stayed that way in silence for several minutes. When he finally spoke, the teasing was gone. "This isn't enough for me, Adria."

Alarm bells jangled inside her at the threat of losing what they wanted so badly to keep. She pulled back and looked up at him. "I'm not sure I know what you mean."

He brushed the curve of her jaw with his thumb. "I want more. You make me want more. More than sex on a picnic table. But what I want isn't the most important thing here."

No, she pleaded silently. Don't do this. Not now. Not yet. Adria had an irrational urge to cover her ears. She didn't want to hear this. *Because he's right*, her inner voice said.

What about what I want? she wanted to shout. Slowly, almost painfully, she withdrew from the comfort and warmth of Dane's embrace.

"Adria—"

She slid awkwardly from his lap and began

putting on her clothes. Funny, she thought. Knowing he watched, she found covering up more disconcerting than exposing herself to him.

Maybe because she was covering up far more than her body. Each article of clothing she donned was like a piece of mental armor.

"Adria." This time it was a command, not a plea.

She turned to see him getting dressed as well. "Don't start telling me about wrong place, wrong time, wrong woman, wrong everything."

He moved so fast, he instantly had her hauled up to his chest, her face held hard with one hand, her hips cemented to his with the other. "Great place, the best time in my life, with the only woman." He kissed her hard until she was gasping for breath and clinging to him. "You got that?"

She managed to nod weakly.

"But I can't do a damn thing about any of it until I take care of the rest. And I can't have you until I do."

"Yeah," she whispered. "I guess I know that. But it doesn't mean I don't hate it."

"I just hope you don't hate me when it's all over."

"That'll never happen," she said with full confidence.

He held her tightly in his arms. "Adria, I'm

getting pressure to close this case. I have other more important cases to get back to."

"Dane, I don't hold you responsible for reporting the facts. But I am innocent of negligence. The only negligent party was that third pilot. We just need time to find the proof."

"Forster expects this report Friday. If I don't have anything concrete by then, I have to give him what I've got. But right now that's not enough to buy more time. And once he turns it over to the FAA, I don't think they'll look any further for a 'make everyone happy' solution than having your job on a platter."

Excitement of a different nature coursed through Adria. "Then let me help you out. After Sarah Greene called me this morning, I searched the *Post* for a follow-up story on Indian Head. There was one, but the byline wasn't hers. Which is very odd. So I went to the *Post* and had someone point her out to me.

"Dane, the reason I called you today was to tell you that the Sarah Greene I met at the playground, the Sarah Greene who called me on the phone, is not the Sarah Greene who works at the *Post*."

EIGHT

"Damn, damn, damn." Dane didn't care if Forster, who had just left his office, heard him.

Since Adria had dropped her little bomb on him yesterday, he'd been working nonstop. Hell, if he were honest, he'd admit that the information about the fake *Post* reporter was the smallest of the bombs she'd dropped on him yesterday. A picnic table, for Christ's sake.

And he'd loved every damn second of it. If he had half a chance, he'd do it again. And again. Here. There.

But now he had no chance. Forster had seen to that.

"How in the hell am I going to tell her?"

"Tell me what?"

Adria stood in the doorway. Anxious with the most absurd fear that she could tell what he'd just been thinking, he watched as she walked over to his cluttered desk.

"You haven't slept or shaved since you left me yesterday, have you?" She peered at the overflowing trash can. "Or eaten. You're living on caffeine."

And memories, he thought. "I came back and began running checks on our Ms. Greene. I've been at it ever since."

She looked as if she wanted to say something. Something personal. Not now, he thought. If it killed him he would keep this meeting business. Hell, by the time he told her about his meeting with Forster, he wouldn't have to worry about talking to her at all. "I still haven't been able to find out who she really is. But I did learn from a member of the recovery crew that she had flashed credentials and used Forster's name. Which doesn't mean squat. It's not impossible to get Forster's name and fake IDs."

Adria sank down into a visitor's chair. "I've been racking my brain all night and I just can't figure out what this woman's agenda is. She pretends to be a reporter to grill me and try to find out what I know about the investigation. She learns I'm most likely the fall guy, then I don't hear from her again. All of a sudden she pops up on national television, digging around looking for plane parts." Adria leaned forward and snagged the open Coke on Dane's desk, absently helping herself to a deep swallow.

It was such a casual gesture, Dane thought, one not unusual between two people who'd been as intimate as they had been. Maybe that was why it hit him so hard. It was the only indication either of them had given since yesterday that anything had happened between them at all.

Maybe it was just as well, his little voice commented. And maybe you can go to hell, he shot back silently.

"It's all circumstantial," he said finally. He held up his hand to forestall her argument. "I agree that there is a bunch of it, but I ran what I had past Forster, hoping he'd give me more time."

"And?" Adria immediately shook her head. "Never mind. I can read it on your face."

When had he let the rest of his guard fall around her? Masking his emotions was second nature for him. It was his *entire* nature. It made him a good investigator. Plane crashes were brutal, ugly scenes of carnage and death. A little detachment went a long way. And he'd taken detachment to a whole new level. Until Adria.

"Don't worry, Dane. I know this makes you uncomfortable. I'm not trying to make you more so, believe me."

"That's just it," he said. "I do believe you.

About everything." And she deserved to know. He hadn't been trying to save *her* the pain, he'd been trying to save himself.

"Well, then," she said, sitting up straighter, clasping her hands in her lap. "I guess we have our work cut out for us, don't we?"

"What do you mean?"

"I know you don't think you need my help on this, but it's my job on the line. I promise I won't do anything to compromise yours, no matter what happens. But we have to find evidence and I'm convinced our reporter is the link. Friday is less than three days away. You can't expect me to just sit around twiddling my thumbs. I won't. I can't."

He was a dead man. Death right now would be preferable to what he was about to tell her. *You're a coward, Dane Colbourne.*

He'd never thought that of himself before. But maybe it was because he'd never risked anything of real importance to himself.

"We don't have until Friday, Adria. We don't have any time at all."

She froze. Then, so quietly it hurt, she said, "What do you mean?"

Dane stood and came around the desk. When he was a step from her, she shifted away.

That withdrawal ripped into him, and he stilled for half a second. Then, as casually as possible, he rested his hip on the desk, folding his arms on his chest. The pose hid the tight fists and, he hoped, the similar tight hold he was maintaining on his control. Only the barest thread of it kept him from yanking her into his arms.

"I just had a meeting with Forster," he said. "He wanted an update and made it clear he was impatient. So I told him what I was working on and argued for more time."

He was falling to pieces inside. If Adria was feeling anything the least bit similar, she was doing a good job hiding it. Which scared him. No one was easier to read than Adria Burke.

"I take it Mr. Forster didn't think an unexplained third plane, a spy running around posing as a reporter, and threatening phone calls to one of the major players in this case warranted any suspicion or concern. Or any more of your precious time." Her tone had been as cool and calm as her blue eyes.

He wanted to beg her to yell and scream. He certainly wanted to yell and scream himself.

"He wants my report today. Facts only, no supposition."

"And you don't find this odd? This rush job, I mean?"

He dug his fingertips harder into his palms. "Adria, I don't know—" He pushed off his desk and stood in front of her chair. She tilted her head to maintain direct eye contact.

"I will admit that it's unusual for Forster to put this kind of pressure on me. But I have two other cases I've been working on, and he feels this is the least problematic of them. He wants it wrapped up now."

"Can't he just reassign it to another investigator?"

No! Dane was amazed he'd kept from shouting it out loud. The truth was, he didn't want any other man sniffing around in Adria's business or in her life, period. So he would let her take the fall for something he knew in his gut she wasn't responsible for? *You're a real prince, Colbourne.*

"You have lousy taste in men," he muttered, more to himself than to her. She gasped. "I'm sorry." He almost laughed at the understatement, but instead added, "About so many things." She paled, obviously misunderstanding him.

He cringed. Just once he wanted to say the right thing. And if that didn't happen now, he might never have another chance.

He reached for her. "Come here," he said softly. He gave her no choice, afraid of the one she'd make if he let her, knowing he had to have her in his arms to be able to explain. To her. To himself.

She allowed him to hold her, but her body

was stiff. He ran a finger along her jaw to her chin, prodding it upward until she met his gaze. What he saw in her eyes wasn't reassuring.

"I know you weren't negligent, Adria."

"Then help me prove it."

"I've spent every spare minute and a whole bunch I didn't have trying to do just that. I have no choice about turning in my report. The other investigators are as overburdened as I am. Forster won't budge. He's used to giving orders and having them followed. And once he turns it in to the FAA . . ." There was no need to go on; the pain in her eyes told him.

"Then I guess I'll just have to keep digging on my own," she said. By the time the FAA is ready to move on this, I'll be ready." He must have looked skeptical, because she lifted her chin from his finger and challenged him with a glacial stare.

"I have to, Dane. Don't you see? Otherwise I have nothing."

"You have me." He sucked in his breath, fear lancing through him. Had he really said that? Opened himself up for the rejection she was sure to deliver? Would the pain of her rejection even remotely pay him back for the pain he'd caused her by letting her down?

"Do I really?" she whispered. "I need you. In ways that scare me to even think about. But if you can stand here and tell me that you're prepared and willing to turn in a report that doesn't have *all* the facts thoroughly investigated and reported, that you're satisfied with the job you've done here, then you aren't the man I thought you were. If that's the man you're offering me, I don't want him. I deserve better than that."

Dane would have sworn he felt his heart break—if he did have one.

"I guess I don't have a choice then, do I?" His attempt at a smile was a travesty. "What's the worst the old bastard can do? Fire me?"

Adria's cheeks burned like a slap in the face when she realized what she'd really just asked of him. When had self-protection changed to self-centeredness? Her job was on the line and that was all that had mattered to her. Looking out for number one and making sure everyone else looked out for her too.

She hadn't taken even one second to wonder if by disobeying his boss, he would be jeopardizing his job. Was that something she could honestly ask him to do? Especially when she knew that he felt as strongly about his career as she did about hers.

"No," she said. "There has to be another way. I can't let you risk your job either."

"Adria—"

"No, Dane, I didn't think. I should never have—"

He didn't give her a chance to finish. His

mouth covered hers swiftly and surely. He held her head and moved his lips over hers, twined his tongue with hers, until she could no longer remember anything except how wonderful he tasted and how much she'd have missed never having him make her feel this way again.

He finally lifted his mouth and let his forehead rest on hers. "You're right. You deserve better than me. I made you a promise, that I'd find the truth. And yet the moment I get an order, it's like I'm one of Pavlov's dogs. 'Sorry, but duty calls.' I would have kept looking—on my own time, I'd have helped you, but it's a poor excuse. I'm sorry. I've always been so sure that I control the system and make it work for me, I never realized just when I became the system."

He leaned down and kissed her again, his touch almost reverent. "You humble me." At her confused expression, he said, "I have no doubt that you'd have gone to the wire for a colleague, for anyone you felt was being wronged—" He broke off, his eyes widening as if he'd just solved a puzzle. "That's what the reprimands were about. You were taking the rap for someone else. Why, Adria?"

Adria didn't answer for a while. "It was Pete Moore," she finally muttered.

"What is Pete Moore to you that you'd risk blemishing your work history?"

Adria wasn't sure what motivated the new tension in his voice, but she was certain she shouldn't be intrigued by the possibility that it might be jealousy. But it did take the edge off her reply. "Pete is a man going through personal hell. A hell I know all too intimately. He's going through a divorce. Thinking I was helping him, I misguidedly helped him out a few times when fatigue and emotional exhaustion made his judgment a tiny bit foggy."

"You don't have room for those kinds of mistakes in your job, Adria. I can't believe you stood by and allowed the man to put people at risk."

"I didn't stand by, I stepped in and did what I had to do. My mistake was in thinking I was helping Pete. I realized that the night of the incident. He'd let the AirWest and the Liberty get too close together. I noticed it when I took control of my position that night and moved immediately to rectify the situation. But even before the incident occurred, I'd already decided I was going to have a long talk with Pete and convince him to take personal leave and get some help. I should have done that right from the start."

Dane put the rest together quickly. "You spoke to Pete after the incident. Why didn't you tell me? I specifically asked you for a list of who you spoke to that night."

"I didn't talk to him that night. I called

him the next day. Not to tell him about what had happened, but to follow up on my original vow to get him out of the tower. Pete was more resistant than I'd expected, and I got angry. I explained what he'd left me with that night and I guess I mentioned the primary target plane." She paused for a moment, the heated emotion of her long conversation with Pete playing back through her mind. "He was upset, but he was convinced his job was all he had left keeping him sane. He swore he'd do better, get more rest."

"Adria," Dane warned.

"I didn't let him get away with it. I eventually issued him an ultimatum: Either he take leave and get counseling, or I'd report him for negligence."

Dane nodded, clearly respecting and understanding how difficult that had been for her. "Do you think he was angry enough to contact the media and try to point the finger at you? Could he have mentioned the target plane not knowing it hadn't been discussed outside your talks with Beck and me?"

Adria thought about it for a moment, then shook her head. "I don't think so. But if our intrepid spy-slash-reporter was covering all her bases, she might have known enough to contact Pete and ask questions. The state he's in, it wouldn't have been too hard to get him to reveal what I'd told him. I didn't caution him against it; it didn't occur to me that I had to. He knows the rules."

"Ms. Greene, or whoever she is, could have told him she was from my office. He might have assumed he was talking on the record for the investigation."

Adria nodded. "That makes sense. And I guess she didn't use the same ruse with me because she knew I'd been questioned too closely by you." She snorted and hung her head. "Not to mention I gave her the perfect cover by assuming out loud that she was the *Post* reporter."

"You had no way of knowing." Dane was silent for a moment, then released her and turned to his desk. "I wish we could figure out who the hell she is. I spent all night going through every database I have access to and a few I don't. I called in favors, used contacts I haven't used in years. No one knows this woman."

Adria had started to reach for him, intent on rubbing his shoulders. Her hand stilled in front of her. She felt like slime as she took in the strain and tension that lined his weary face. "I owe you an apology. You were wrong earlier. You have no reason to be humbled. Certainly not by me. I shouldn't have said what I did about the kind of man you are. I know what kind of man you are. I'm sure I've always known. You've gone above and beyond what other investigators would have. Most of them would have listened politely to my explanation on the highly improbable third-plane scenario, and it would have ended there. Certainly when the ARTS tapes were reviewed. Even before we . . . became involved, you were already helping me. You'd have done the same for anyone you thought might shed light on the facts. On the truth."

"Adria—"

"I owe you for going as far as you have. I'm scared and angry and I hate feeling trapped like this by the system, but I had no right—"

"Adria, I *am* the system." He pressed a finger to her lips to keep her from going on. "But this time I can't make the rules work for me. Or for you." He moved away from the desk, his lips pulling back until two rows of white teeth were exposed in the most devilishly sexy grin she'd ever seen. "So, I say it's about time we broke a few." He stopped less than a breath away. "How about it? You up for a little aviation espionage?"

Right now Adria would have settled for air. "I should never have taught you how to smile like that," she whispered.

His chuckle was rusty, but it made her shiver all over. His hands settled on her hips and he gently tugged her forward until they bumped his.

"So, are we a team?" The rough quality to his voice made her think of all sorts of teamwork she'd like to indulge in with this man.

She nodded.

"Good. But first I really need to do this." He slid his hands up her back and pulled her fully against him. Just before his mouth covered hers, he whispered, "I won't let you down again, Adria. I swear it."

NINE

Adria fumbled with her house keys, conscious of Dane right behind her. Even though they'd driven separate cars, she'd been aware of him since they'd left his office.

That kiss . . . Something had changed between them. It was as if his whispered vow carried a much deeper commitment.

She really hadn't given much thought to what would happen between them after the case was over. Now she did.

She finally managed to open her door. "Can I get you something to drink," she asked as she entered.

"The usual. Thanks," he said. Adria was warmed by the smile in his voice. He *had* changed.

"No problem." She dropped her purse and

keys on the foyer table. "If you want to make your calls, I could fix a bite—"

Dane took her elbow and swung her into his arms, against his body. It thrilled her how smoothly, how easily, how perfectly, she moved against him. He closed the door with his back and leaned against it, pulling her with him. She rested between his legs. His mouth came down on hers and she gave to him willingly.

His hands slid down and gripped the curve of her buttocks. "We have to get to work, set plans in motion. . . ." His words trailed off as he brushed kisses along her jaw and down her neck to her shoulder. "And all I can think of is making love to you again."

"Me too. My job is at stake, and I can't stop thinking about . . . wanting to . . ." Her hips arched against his, making her desire clearer than any words could.

Dane groaned. His hands still molding her backside, he pushed from the door and backed her to the stairs. Instead of climbing them, he pressed her down until she was on her back and he lay fully on top of her. She opened her legs, forming a cradle for his hips.

Adria reveled in how readily, how badly she wanted him. How she enjoyed his intensity. His control, his command of her body, was so different, so pleasurable. . . .

She had changed too.

"The bed," he whispered roughly. "I thought it would be nice to make love to you on a bed, but—"

"Next time." She reached for the waistband of his pants. She had his buckle undone and the zipper halfway down when the phone rang. Dane stilled, Adria didn't. "Don't. Let the machine get it."

Bracing his weight on one arm, he pulled her shirt from her pants.

The machine clicked on. "You're kidding yourself if you think spreading your legs for the investigator will help your cause," the caller said in a low, rough whisper. The gender was difficult to discern.

They both froze.

"Leave it alone," the caller continued. "And leave Colbourne alone. You're in over your head. And his. It's over. You lost."

Dane was across the room before Adria could take a single breath. But the click of the disconnection sounded just as his hand hit the phone. He was too late.

He lifted the receiver anyway, then slammed it back on the base. "Damn!"

Adria jerked into action, yanking her shirt down as she scrambled off the step.

"No!" Dane made a chopping motion with his hand. "Stay where you are."

Adria was so taken aback, she followed without question. She watched, her heart still pounding, only not with passion, as he moved to the side of her front window.

He carefully nudged apart the blinds and scanned the street. "No cars on the curb, two cars in driveways. A red Bronco two doors down, this side of the street, and a gray Honda three doors down across the street."

"Those belong there," she confirmed. "I'll check from upstairs, the view is better." She half expected him to stop her and demand that he be the one to check.

"Be careful," was all he said.

She knew him well enough to realize his respect wasn't easily won. And apparently he knew her well enough to understand how important it was to her to be taken seriously, to be considered an equal. Her nerves were still jangled, but she found a smile for him. "I will." She climbed up a step. "Not exactly how I expected to end up in my bedroom."

"I remember exactly where we left off." He crossed the room to stand by the stairs. All business now, he said, "After you check the backstreet, I want you to throw a few things together. I don't think it's safe to stay here."

She didn't either. "I guess we can go to a hotel."

He shook his head. "No hotels. If this person is tracing your every move, they'll figure it out."

"So where do we go?"

"To my place."

"That's safer? It's the first place they'll look."

"I don't intend to stay there, but I have to contact someone who can help us out and get a few things as well."

She nodded. "Okay, I trust you."

"I won't forget that either." She took another step, but he stopped her by putting a hand on hers. The warmth of his skin, the strength in his fingers, comforted her.

"Don't use a suitcase, just a large handbag or something."

She nodded again, not trusting herself to speak, and ran quickly up the stairs.

"Who is Jarrett McCullough?"

Dane was thankful that was all Adria asked. He didn't want to have to explain the cryptic message he'd just left on Jarrett's answering machine.

"He's a friend. The best."

He scooped up his Coke and notes and sat on a barstool across the room from Adria. She was curled up on the end of his couch nursing an iced tea.

He'd chosen the couch as he'd chosen everything else in his house—for comfort and utility. Now he had to admit the place did look a bit drab. If what was surfacing in him was some latent urge to decorate, at least he'd started with the best room brightener he could think of. Adria.

She studied him for a moment. "You don't have too many friends, I'd wager," she said.

He tried to look affronted. He wasn't too keen that she'd realized just how easily he shut most people out. Even his sister's well-meaning teasing hadn't woken him up to that fact.

"You're intimating I don't play well with others?"

"Not at all. But I can't see you letting anyone too close either. In fact, I'll bet ten to one you've known Jarrett since you were kids, before your walls were too high to scale. He's one of the Musketeers you mentioned, isn't he?"

He glanced at the table that doubled for his desk over in the corner of the small living room. It was cluttered with open books, charts, piles of folders, mangled plane parts. And one photo. He looked back at her.

She wasn't the least bit repentant. "So I glanced at your 'collection' while you were fixing my tea. Call it professional curiosity."

He thought of all the things he wanted to share with her, none of them remotely professional in nature. "Those plane parts don't belong in my collection. They're bits and pieces of ongoing investigations. Most of what I've kept is at work."

It went unsaid that since he spent most of his time there, it made sense to keep any personal mementos there. But he knew she didn't judge him wanting because of that.

The tension eased out of him slowly; his body relaxed. He let out a long, slow breath as he drank in the sight of her. She made him feel as if he'd been holding his breath all his life . . . waiting. For her.

"Who's the other boy in the photo?"

"Zach Brogan." His smile was slight, but he was enjoying the instant reaction he always got from Adria when he tried one out, so he was making an effort to do it more often. "He just married the girl in the photo." The smile broadened a bit more easily. "My twin sister, Dara."

"Your twin?"

He'd surprised her. "You say that like you feel sorry for the world in general that there are two of us."

She shook her head. "No, not at all. Something about the way she's looking at the three of you tells me she was probably the only person who kept you guys in line."

Dane stepped over to the desk. He didn't have to look at the picture to know every individual grain of color in it. He picked it up and crossed to the couch. Adria lowered her feet to the floor and Dane sat close beside her, holding the photo so they could both look at it.

"This was taken the summer before my dad died. He was the one who took it. Zach and I had found this old spring out on Jarrett's farm property."

"Where was this?"

"Madison County, right smack in front of the Blue Ridge Mountains."

"Looks beautiful." She traced a finger over the tree and small watering hole to the side of the cluster of tanned, smiling kids.

"It was. I figured out how to get the spring dug out and Zach constructed the rope swing on the tree. It took almost all summer before the water got deep enough to swim in, but that August we spent every day out there." He smiled at the memories. "The Three Musketeers."

"Four," Adria put in, pointing at Dara.

Dane shot her a wry look. "My sister would love you."

"I bet she didn't let a little male chauvinism slow her down one bit."

Dane tensed a little. "No, not Dara. She was knocked hard for a loop when Dad died. She's lost a few heroes in her life."

"And Zach?"

Dane's laugh was still rusty, but it felt good. "Loves her so much it makes me sick."

"Said like a true brother."

"Zach Brogan was the last man Dara ever thought would be a hero. She'd pretty much closed herself off."

"Like you?" she asked.

"Yeah. But for different reasons." He paused, then said, "Actually, Zach is about the last guy I'd have ever chosen for my brother-in-law."

Adria's eyes widened at the slight edge to his tone. "Why? I thought he was your best friend too?"

Dane shook his head, feeling awkward as he realized just how many levels there were to real intimacy. In a way, he felt more vulnerable now than he had been naked by the picnic table. "He still is," he said finally. "Zach is a thrill seeker, by blood and by profession. Let's just say that I'd trust him to get me off a mile-high cliff without a scratch, but I wouldn't trust him with my sister."

"Also spoken like a true brother." She added, "Which, considering I don't have one, makes my opinion worth nil on this subject, I guess. But if he loves her, then it can't be too bad a match."

"No," he admitted. "It's not. In fact, it's great and I'm happy for both of them. Dara's happier than I've ever seen her."

"I take it they're newlyweds?"

"Do you think I wear white tuxedos for kicks?"

Adria grinned broadly. "I'm sorry you had to be called away from such a momentous occasion. Although I guess it's not the first time."

Dane remembered how odd he'd felt as Zach and Dara had said their vows. Proud, happy, confused . . . lonely. He'd chalked it up to having watched Jarrett say those same words not a month or so earlier. He was the last unattached Musketeer.

Not that he wanted to be attached, or envied Zach and Jarrett, he'd told himself.

He looked at Adria—and questioned every decision he'd ever made about his life as a single man.

"Is Jarrett married now too?"

"Yes. The wedding was a few months ago."

The silence that spun out between them thrummed with anticipation. Dane had no idea what he was waiting for. He started to stand, intent on returning the picture and getting back to mapping out their strategy. She held him back with a simple hand on his arm.

"I bet it's strange having your foundation altered so swiftly," she said. "Maybe you don't even think about them, or see them that often. But they are your closest friends, and, in many ways, you define yourself by your personal relationships. Then they make this big change, and suddenly nothing's the same anymore."

"You're spooky, you know that?"

She shook her head. "Nah. I may not have siblings or childhood buddies, but I know how I felt when I lost my grandfather, then my father. I know how it altered how I thought of myself, and therefore how I thought of Tony."

"Death is a lot more profound than marriage. Not to mention permanent. I still have Zach and Jarrett in my life."

She let her hand slide down to his, let her fingers rest between his. "True. You're lucky. Don't lose sight of that."

Dane twined his fingers with hers. He didn't have to tug too hard to get her to move closer. Another little tug and she was in his arms. He kissed her, slowly, leisurely, memorizing her lips, her taste. He wanted to savor it. Save it.

"Yes," he whispered against that spot below her ear. "I'm just beginning to realize how lucky I am."

Adria was starting to writhe beneath him when the phone rang. Dane swore. "This is getting ridiculous."

Adria was breathless, but said, "At least we hadn't taken our clothes off."

"I'm beginning to doubt if I'll ever have that distinct pleasure again." The phone rang a third time and his machine picked up. Adria stiffened beneath him. He pulled her closer, wrapping an arm around her, the protective urge instantaneous. That she let him bright-ened his mood a little.

"Aramis, Athos here," said the caller.

Adria heaved a sigh of obvious relief. Dane reached for the portable phone without letting her go. "That was fast," he said into the phone.

"I'm on my honeymoon. This better be life or death, buddy."

"Why do I get the feeling I could have called ten months from now and gotten the same answer?"

Jarrett chuckled. "Yeah, well, sue me."

The ache that had been in Dane's chest since the night his sister had taken her vows eased slightly. He was truly happy for both his friends and their wives. And not so confused anymore either, he thought when Adria's hand crept into his.

"You know how I love fairy-tale endings," Dane said soberly, turning to the matter at hand.

"Yeah. Always seems to be another dragon, though, you know?"

"You got it. Always another Rapunzel in the tower, looking to get out."

"Where's a good safe castle when you need one, eh?"

"My thoughts exactly."

"You talk to Porthos?"

"Nah. D'Artagnan would kill me."

Another rusty chuckle. "Yeah, if Porthos didn't first." There was a pause, then: "I don't think Sleeping Beauty here will mind too much." There was a squeal on the other end just before the phone was muffled.

Dane felt his neck heat.

A moment later Jarrett spoke again. "Remember the summer of eighty-nine?"

Dane thought back. The three of them had met out past Culpepper in the middle of the night to get an early start on a climbing trip. Only Zach would consider parasails standard mountain-hiking equipment. It had been one helluva weekend.

"Yes," he answered. "And so does my back."

"Same time, same place."

"Thanks." It had been a long time since he'd asked anything of his friends. And lately he hadn't been much of a participant in Musketeer adventures. "I wouldn't have called, but this one . . . I owe you."

"It's about time, Aramis. Or should I say Romeo?"

Dane grinned and tightened his hold on Adria. "Must be contagious."

"D'Artagnan might have forgiven you for this one."

"One step at a time, brother, one step at a time."

"I hear you. But I'm here to say, happily

ever after is pretty damn good. Take care of yourself." He hung up.

This peaceful, content Jarrett was not the intensely driven, private person Dane had grown up with. He almost felt guilty for dragging Jarrett back into the intrigue business. But he'd had no choice. Jarrett still had the second-best contacts on earth.

The person with the first best was his next call.

"Everything okay with Athos?" Adria asked.

Considering their intimate journey into his past, Dane didn't doubt for a moment Adria had figured out his part of the coded conversation with Jarrett.

"Better than all right. Although it doesn't feel too good asking the guy to help."

"You'd do the same for him."

"Yes, I would. But it's not the same. Not anymore. He has someone besides himself to worry about."

Matching his seriousness, Adria said, "I appreciate all you're doing for me. I imagine asking for help isn't on your list of favorite things to do. If there was any way I could pay you back—"

Dane cut her off with a shake of his head. He reached up and brushed back several wayward strands of hair from her cheeks. "Maybe he and I have more in common than I realized."

"Dane, I can take care of myself. Don't—"

"I don't want anything to happen to you," he said, his voice suddenly tight. He cleared his throat. "I don't know how this is all going to shake out. Whether you'll want to be with me a week from now, a month from now." She looked as if she had wondered the same thing. "But I do know I want to make love to you again. On a bed, on the floor, against the wall. In the kitchen, the bedroom, and at twenty thousand feet in a sky that matches your eyes." She gasped and his body went rock hard in response. "I want to know about the stories your dad told you at our picnic table, your granddad's time in a DC-3, and why you became the best air-traffic controller the Mike Munroney Aeronautical Center has ever graduated." He pushed his fingers into her hair, cupping her head as he tilted her face to his. "I want you. All of you."

Her mouth was less than a breath away from his. "Then make that other call and get this thing moving." Her lips brushed his as she spoke. "Because I want those very same things and I don't want any more distractions."

"I'm calling, I'm calling," he said, but he was kissing her. He couldn't not kiss her.

Their passion rapidly escalated until Adria nudged Dane away. "This is insane. You, me, those creepy phone calls." She shivered and Dane drew her more tightly against him. "I just want it over. One way or the other. I'm not too sure I even care about the third plane at this point."

Dane relaxed his hold on her. "Yes, you do. You're just tired and spooked and worried about losing a job you've given your life to. What's happening between us isn't lessening the confusion." When he started to move away, she grabbed his arms, her grip strong, but he didn't let her talk. "Maybe we should cool things down. Maybe I should be doing my job and letting you focus your energies on that damn plane and on keeping your job."

"Maybe so," she said. "But life doesn't hand us things in neat little packages, you know. We just get it hurled at us in ungainly globs."

Despite his best intentions, Dane gave in to her teasing. "I'm not sure I like being an 'ungainly glob.'"

Adria traced his face with her fingers, spending a painfully long, body-tightening time on his lips. "Yeah, but you're *my* ungainly glob." He bared his teeth and playfully nipped at her finger. "Do you really think it's necessary to do all this cloak-and-dagger stuff? I mean, I could do the scarf-and-sunglasses bit and check into a local hotel for a few days while you get your last source to run down our fake reporter."

"I wouldn't have contacted Jarrett if I didn't think it was necessary. I'm not too comfortable with you even being here this long. I've got the feeling your every move—and quite possibly mine—is being monitored. I don't want to take any chances."

"Even the phones? That was the reason for all that fairy-tale Musketeer mumbo jumbo right?"

"I just have a bad feeling about this. Better safe than sorry."

Adria was silent for a moment, then said, "Okay, so, who is this last source person?"

Dane's lips quirked. "Her name is Beaudine Delacroix and she'd cane me if she heard herself referred to as a 'last' anything."

"She must be quite a woman to intimidate 'the Predator.' "

Dane didn't disagree. "She works for Zach. Dara calls her a Cajun Mrs. Doubtfire. She's the most amazing woman I've ever met in my life." He dropped a quick kiss on her lips. "Present company excepted."

Lips tingling, Adria asked, "How long will it take to get through to her?"

"Not long at all."

"And what time do we rendezvous with 'Athos'?"

"Midnight."

A wicked look gleamed in Adria's eyes. "That should leave us plenty of time."

"For what?" he asked, though his body was already ten steps ahead on the right track.

Adria freed the top two buttons of his shirt. "Make the call, then I'll show you."

"Adria," Dane warned, knowing all their energies should be devoted exclusively to the case right now. For both their sakes one of them should play bad cop right now.

She slipped her hand inside his shirt.

He made the call.

TEN

Just before nine o'clock, there was a knock on the door. Adria froze, her gaze locked on Dane's as he sat across from her at the small table in his kitchen. They had spent the better part of the evening going over his files and his preliminary findings. It had been an exercise in frustration. There wasn't a trace of hard evidence to support her claim.

"You expecting anyone?" she whispered.

Dane shook his head as the rapping came again. A finger to his lips, he slid from his chair and made his way to the door.

"Aramis, you in, ol' buddy?"

Adria saw the tension ease immediately from Dane's shoulders and back. He quickly opened the door and ushered in the unexpected guest. "What the hell are you doing here?" he demanded, but his expression made it clear he wasn't disappointed by the appearance of the tall, blond man.

Adria couldn't see the stranger's face, but she definitely saw his form. And he was no slouch. Tall and well muscled, he planted big fists on jean-clad hips.

"I'm here on Damsel Detail," he announced cheerfully. Obviously Dane's less-than-cordial greeting hadn't affected him in the least. Then he turned, directing his cocky grin right at her. "You must be the damsel."

He stalked across the room and stuck his hand out. "Hi, I'm Zach Brogan." He shot an amused look back at Dane, who had followed him. "Or is that Porthos?"

Dane scowled. "Beaudine has a big mouth."

"As wide as a Cajun moon, my friend," he said. "Or should I say, brother?"

That got an abashed smile from Dane. Zach just laughed and turned his attention back to Adria.

Adria shook Zach's hand, immediately liking this big bear of a man. "Pleased to meet you. I'm Adria Burke." She added, "The damsel."

Zach was clearly impressed. "Yeah, you'll do." To Dane, he said, "Did you really think Beaudine would let you and McCullough have all the fun and leave me out?"

"You just got back from your honeymoon.

I didn't think you'd appreciate the interruption. How is my sister anyway? Did she survive the trip?"

Zach laughed. He was more than a little overwhelming—in size and sheer presence. Adria imagined Dara had to be some woman to have captured the heart of this man.

"She was amazing. Almost killed me." He waggled his eyebrows. "And that was before I got her to fly the glider."

Dane went on alert. "Dara flew? A glider?"

"I know how much she missed it as a kid, after your dad died," he said quietly. "I guess I figured something without an engine might be less scary."

Dane shook his head, obviously amazed. "Only you would use that kind of logic. How'd she do?"

"She loved it, man. I'll never forget the instant she pulled the tow release and she was on her own. She was like an eagle."

"I owe you for life for giving that back to her," Dane said. "Thank you." He faltered for a moment, then added, "Welcome to the family."

Adria teared up when the two men embraced briefly.

"Where is she, anyway?" Dane asked. "You didn't tell her about this, did you? I don't want her to—"

Zach waved a hand. "Not to worry. She's

on a three-day trip with a group of the Dream Foundation kids. Disney World."

"And you didn't go along?" Dane taunted.

Zach cleared his throat and with mock manly swagger said, "Nah, too amateur for a pro like me. Actually, she was afraid I'd get them all kicked out of the park for doing something crazy."

"Can't imagine why," Dane deadpanned.

Zach laughed. "Yeah. I miss her like hell, though. I've got Scotty handling most of the trips and I'm interviewing to bring on another guide." He slapped Dane on the shoulder. "In the meantime you get to provide some entertainment."

He turned to Adria.

"You ready to rock-and-roll, Rapunzel?"

Adria couldn't help herself. She had to say it. "How in the world did you two hook up as kids? You're as different as Dumas's Musketeers could ever hope to be."

Zach stared at Dane, who looked distinctly uncomfortable under the scrutiny. "You told her about us as kids?" He looked like a bad boy who'd just been handed the perfect snowball. "So, it's like that."

"Zach—" The warning in Dane's voice was edged in cold steel and would have sent other men stumbling over themselves in apology. Not Zach.

"Beaudine just scored another bonus. She

figured it just from one phone call. I had to see it to believe it." He shook his head. "The woman must have voodoo in her family tree."

Adria looked back and forth between the two men. She'd understood that Dane didn't share his personal life, much less his past, with just anyone. But it was clear that Dane hadn't realized how obvious he'd been to his friends. Should she waste a moment trying to deflect Zach's interest in the exact nature of her relationship with Dane? The fact of the matter was, she didn't really know what the nature of their relationship was at this point.

Zach spied her backpack on the floor near the door and crossed the room to scoop it up. "Where's the rest of it?"

There wasn't anything else, but Adria didn't answer immediately. She'd caught Dane watching her in that intent way of his that made her forget about the rest of the universe.

He didn't move and neither did she. They simply held each other's gaze, communicating silently.

Seconds later—or it could have been hours—Zach cleared his throat. "We'd better get this show on the road. Jarrett, er, Athos, is waiting." Dane glared at him. "What made you dredge up those nicknames anyway?"

Dane shrugged. "I had to get a message to Jarrett and I wasn't sure how secure my phone lines were, so I improvised. Hey, I'm not the secret-agent man of the trio here. I did my best."

"And a fine job it was," Zach responded, doffing an imaginary hat and bowing in the best Musketeer tradition. Adria was thoroughly amused.

When Zach straightened, she shoved her chair back and stood. "I guess I'm ready." She nodded to the backpack that looked tiny in Zach's big hands. "That's it."

Zach's eyes widened. "Dane, where did you find this rare gem?" He turned back to Adria. "His sister packs for a weekend camping trip like she's outfitting a major expedition. Maybe you two could get together and—"

"Hey," Dane said, "why don't we worry about getting her safe before we plan the future."

Adria tensed at his sharp tone. Before she or Zach could comment, Dane blew out a sigh. "Sorry."

Adria didn't want him to worry about her, but she couldn't deny how glad she was that he did.

Dane's gaze stayed riveted on hers, but his next words were for Zach. "Take care of her for me."

Zach sobered. "You know I will. Jarrett will contact you when she's in."

Adria asked Dane, "You're not coming?"

"Zach can get you out of here a hundred

different ways I'd never think of. If anyone tailed you here, they won't know you've gone."

"But that leaves you—"

"Don't worry about me. I'm going in to work early tomorrow as usual. Anyone watching me will be bored senseless by nine A.M. If they decide to come here, hoping to find you alone, they'll be disappointed. I'll stall Forster as long as I can without making it obvious I have no intention of filing that report. Let's hope Beaudine comes through before it gets that far. If I can get something tangible linking this woman to the incident, Forster has to let me stay on it. Information like that can be leaked and he knows it."

Heedless of Zach's presence, Adria crossed the room until she stood right in front of Dane. "I really hate being taken out of this. But even more, I hate leaving you in it."

"We agreed that it'll be easier to figure out what's going on without you looking over your shoulder every second. At this point I'm the only one who can get any information. I need to know you're okay, that you're safe."

Her heart was like a fist lodged in her throat. "You told me you were the best and that I should trust you. So I'm going to trust you and do as I'm told."

"I thought you gave that up along with what's-his-name?" he said quietly.

Tenderness from this very tough, very private man who guarded his emotions so carefully, was a very special gift indeed. "Maybe I just didn't like what he was telling me."

"Kiss me."

"See what I mean?" Her hands trembled as she lifted them up to frame his face. Rising to her tiptoes, she kissed him on the mouth, pouring into him all the turbulent emotions the weeks' events had wrought inside her.

He took them all, as fully and deeply as he did her kiss. And gave equally in return. Adria let herself go, reveling in the security she'd found in the circle of his arms. Reveling perhaps because this time she suspected he drew the same comfort from hers.

"Don't do anything macho," she said in a rough whisper against his neck.

"Not unless you're there to witness it and be properly impressed." His voice was as choked with emotion as hers had been, which made his attempt at humor all the more sweet.

"There is hope, Colbourne."

"Yes," he said soberly. "There is. Hold on to it for me, okay?"

Dane was at his desk bright and early the following morning, typing up the beginnings of a formal report that he planned to add to the collected data files. If Forster dropped in, all would look as if Dane was following orders. But Forster hadn't dropped in or called or contacted him in any way since their phone conversation yesterday. Dane had a bad feeling about that.

He tossed his second empty Coke can of the day into the trash can and tried to convince himself that Forster's absence gave Beaudine more time to dig.

Jarrett had sent Zach back in person with the information on Adria's location, which, to Dane's distinct discomfort, turned out to be Jarrett and Rae's mountain cabin. He didn't like having his friends put themselves all out for him. But he had to admit, no one was probably safer than Adria at this moment with two of the finest intelligence minds watching over her.

His phone buzzed. He scooped it up before the second ring. "Colbourne."

"Hey, this is Eliot. I got something I think you might be interested in."

Dane immediately went on full alert. Eliot had been on the team recovering the fuselage. "What's up?"

"Someone phoned in about another piece of fuselage yesterday afternoon. Two pieces actually. It wasn't close to the Indian Head site. Couple found them when they had one of their big tree's pruned."

Tension crept into Dane's every pore,

along with hope. Hope had been the first emotion he'd learned to subordinate long ago. Adria had been the one to bring it to the surface again. And he felt helpless against its power. "Can you tag it as AirWest or Liberty?"

"Definitely came off the Liberty."

The disappointment was so keen he had to swallow a groan of frustration. "Send it over to the warehouse to be cataloged with the rest. I appreciate the call."

"That's not all," Eliot said. "There's some foreign coating on both pieces that didn't come from the AirWest or any other commercial aircraft I know."

Adrenaline kicked in hard like a punch to his entire system. Dane welcomed it. "Describe it."

"It's a flat black, some sort of titanium base, I think. My money would be on military. Though I can't say I've ever seen this particular material before."

"Anything else?" Dane asked.

"Well . . ."

"What've you got?" Dane ordered, that bad feeling coming over him again.

"I called your office with this the moment I found out yesterday, but you weren't in. I was going to page you, but I was rerouted to Forster."

"Forster?" The dread grew.

"Yeah, I thought it was bit odd too. He told me you'd finished the report and had gone back to the Cairo thing. He said he'd pass along the information to you after getting a look at the fuselage himself. I guess he didn't call you."

Dane was beginning to suspect Forster never would have. "You turned the piece over to him?"

"No. I just now got it into the warehouse."

Dane released a deep sigh of relief. "Good, hold on to it for me."

"Uh, well, Forster is due in here any minute to look at it."

That explained why Dane hadn't heard or seen the man today. "Did you tell him about the foreign coating on the pieces?"

"Yes. I asked him if they'd reopen the investigation if this proved to be anything and he said he'd assign someone to it. I got the impression he didn't think it would get that far."

Dane frowned at the news. Even if he made certain word got out about this new evidence, Forster would just reopen the case and assign it to someone else, a green agent he could intimidate into doing whatever his personal agenda dictated. It would be very believable that Dane had been pulled off because his expertise was needed on more crucial matters.

Why had he been given the case in the first

place? Forster must have assigned it before he realized what had happened. Which brought up more questions. What, exactly, was Forster's personal agenda in this matter? Just who was involved in this? And, most important, what really *had* happened in the sky that night over D.C.?

"I really appreciate the heads-up on this, Eliot."

"Sure."

Eliot obviously realized something was fishy, but Dane was reluctant to pull him in any deeper. Unfortunately, he didn't have that luxury. "I need you to do something for me. Send one of the pieces to the lab before Forster shows up. Put my name on the request."

Eliot didn't hesitate. "You got it."

"Let me know the instant you get any word. Page me, don't call."

A slight pause followed this time, but Eliot didn't ask any questions. He just said, "Sure, I'll do my best," and disconnected the call.

"That's all any of us can do," Dane muttered as he hung up.

Just as quickly he lifted the phone again and dialed a familiar number. It was picked up after the first ring.

"The Great Escape."

"Beaudine, it's Dane. I have some information that might help you out."

"Well, *chère*, I can use all the help you got to give. I'm comin' up a total blank on this woman."

"How are your military connections?"

There was a low chuckle. "You don' want to know that for real, *chère*. Which branch?"

"I'm not sure, but I figure the air force is a safe bet. We found some fuselage of the AirWest with some interesting paint on it. Flat, black, made out of material not used on commercial planes."

"I hear you. I'll page you when I know."

"Thanks, Beaudine. I owe you one." He paused. "Even if you did tell Zach."

"And let the boy miss his fun?" She made a tsking sound. "Besides, since your sister left for Florida he's been pouting and moaning around here driving me crazy. And that was just the first fifteen minutes. You think I was going to pass up a chance to get him outta my hair?"

Dane couldn't help but smile. "Yeah, well, I appreciate it no matter why you did it."

"No problem, *chère*. You just invite me to the wedding, you hear?"

By the time Dane had recovered enough to answer, the line was dead. He hung up and pushed back his chair. If Forster was going to be out for the next hour or so, then it was the perfect time to pay a little visit to the man's desk. Perhaps something there would shed some light on exactly what was going on.

Wedding, he thought as he locked his door and headed for Forster's office. The image of Adria walking toward him down the aisle, white gown flowing, arms full of flowers, her blue eyes shining, her smile wide with anticipation of becoming his wife . . .

His wife.

He felt almost embarrassed by the intense rush of pleasure and pride that filled him at the very idea.

What would it be like to wake up with her in bed beside him every morning? Almost as fine as going to that same bed with her the night before.

Life with Adria . . . Their life. Together. He couldn't think of anything more important or a goal more worth pursuing. There would be no going back into his emotionless void, only forward to freedom. Who would have thought he'd find it by falling in love?

Dane stopped dead in his tracks, causing the people behind him to veer sharply around him. "Sorry," he muttered, not really caring.

Love.

The very word should have sent him running in the opposite direction. But it didn't. It excited him. Energized him.

He started walking again. A few doors from Forster's office, he stopped until the hallway cleared long enough for him to slip inside without being noticed.

Since the door was left unlocked, chances were he wouldn't find anything important. But he started sifting through the folders on the desk anyway. He'd just moved to the stack of files on a nearby credenza when his beeper went off. He silenced it as he unclipped it from his belt. He read the number. *Eliot.* Uh-oh. This soon, it couldn't be welcome news.

Dane left the office without having found a thing related to the military or the incident and headed to the nearest pay phone. He quickly punched in the number of the warehouse. After several rings, the call was finally picked up.

"Colbourne here. Get Eliot on the line."

Almost a minute passed during which every worst-case scenario Dane could think of raced through his mind.

"Eliot here." He sounded somewhat out of breath. "Hey, man, I got the one piece out, the other one is gone."

"Did Forster say anything?"

"That's why I called. He didn't come. He sent an aide."

"Who? What was his name?"

"It was a woman."

Dane gripped the phone tightly. "Average height, brown hair, very short, midforties?" he asked, repeating the description Adria had given him.

"Yeah, that's her. She flashed her ID. Said her name was Mary Ellis. I think I saw her out at Indian Head. You know her?"

"Not as well as I'm going to," Dane muttered under his breath. To Eliot, he said, "Yeah, I think so. I appreciate your keeping me up to date."

"One more thing. I asked where Forster was and she said something about him meeting out at the FAA building with the media."

Dane tensed. "Thanks. Let me know when you hear from metallurgy."

"Will do."

Dane hung up and scanned the lobby. He hated feeling hunted, and didn't appreciate the irony of the Predator's role being reversed.

He had to get in touch with Jarrett. He had to talk to Adria, let her know they were getting closer. *Let her know he loved her*. At the very least he had to tell her there was finally evidence that could prove the existence of the third plane. If Forster didn't destroy it first.

And Forster was talking to the media.

Not without me, Dane thought. He now had enough to convince Forster into giving him more time. And he could think of no better place to do the convincing than in front of the media.

He headed out to his car. There was no

time to call Adria. But that was okay. He'd have more to tell her after he'd had his little chat with the old colonel.

By then, this whole thing might just be over.

ELEVEN

Adria slipped into the bathroom, intent on a long soak in the tub. Rae was out in her shop, crafting another one of her intriguing metal-and-gem creations, and Jarrett had gone on a hike with Wolfman, the couple's adorable husky puppy. If you could call almost forty pounds of barely contained exuberance a puppy.

Adria's hosts made an interesting couple. Rae was friendly and very direct. Jarrett was as intense as Dane, very enigmatic, cordial, but not overt like Zach. Heat almost bounced off the walls whenever Rae and Jarrett got within two feet of each other, underscoring how deeply Dane's absence was affecting Adria.

She switched on the small radio on the shelf above the commode, then flipped through the stack of magazines next to the radio, needing something—anything—to take her mind off Dane and how he was faring in her case.

Under the top magazine, she found a pamphlet on baby names. No one had told Adria a baby was on the way. She thought about the baggy sweats and big T-shirt Rae wore. "Could be," she murmured.

Pamphlet in hand, she stepped into the tub and sank into the warm water. She leafed through the pages, half musing if she'd find any names underlined and, if so, what they'd be. Somehow she ended up picking out names *she* liked. Would Dane like them or hate them? Startled, she almost dropped the book. Baby names? "A bit premature, don't you think?" she asked herself. But as she gently tossed the book on the floor, she found her gaze slipping down to her stomach. She gave in to the urge and let her hand smooth over the area beneath her belly button, wondering what it would feel like to have a child inside of her. Dane's child.

It seemed so right. In fact, she'd admit the whole thing made her feel like grinning madly and hugging herself.

She'd fallen in love with Dane Colbourne.

She squeezed her eyes shut, opened them, then gave in to the satisfied grin. Yep. There was no denying it. Dane was compulsive, able to focus on things to the exclusion of the rest of the world, intent, always right—or thought he was—all the things she'd never look for in a man. Yet she loved them all. Just as she loved the way he turned that focus on her, the way his eyes would lose their remote expression when he looked at her, the way they'd heat up and flash like heat lightning when he was making love to her, or when he just wanted to make love to her. . . .

When this whole thing was over, she decided, come hell or high water, she was taking that man away someplace where they could be all alone, to do whatever they wanted. For as long as it took.

Dear Lord, what was she setting herself up for? But it wasn't as if she had a choice. She fought for what she wanted now. And she wanted Dane Colbourne. "Please want me back," she whispered.

"And now for some late-breaking news."

Mired in her thoughts, Adria barely heard the announcer on the radio.

"Retired Colonel Roy Forster of the National Safety Transportation Board made an announcement today in front of the FAA building that the report on the incident that occurred over Metropolitan Airport several weeks ago, where an AirWest and a Liberty plane clipped wings, has been completed."

Adria sat up so fast water splashed over the edge of the tub and soaked the floor.

Forster's voice filled the small room. "It

appears that the probable cause in this incident is not instrumental or mechanical, but human error on the part of the air-traffic controller on duty that night. Our recommendations are now in the hands of the FAA, who will make the final judgment on this. The controller in question, Ms. Adria Burke, has been suspended from duty since the night of the collision."

Oh no. Adria clambered out of the tub. *What happened? Dane, I have to contact Dane.* She struggled to shut out the voices shouting in her head and listen to the rest of the report.

"I would like to commend our lead investigator in this case, Mr. Dane Colbourne, for his quick, thorough work. Without dedication and commitment like his, this case could have dragged on for months. It was a clear-cut situation almost from the first, but he took the time to look into every aspect of the incident."

The newscaster broke back in. "The investigator Mr. Forster referred to, Dane Colbourne, made an appearance toward the end of the announcement, but didn't make any comments of his own."

It was a good thing the toilet was behind her. She had to sit down.

The newscaster went on to other news, but Adria barely heard it. Her mind screamed with suspicions and doubts while her heart cried no, it couldn't be. Dane wouldn't have manipulated her.

He'd believed in her.

He kept you from interfering in his report.

No! He'd made love to her. Revealed things about himself to her, shared more than his body with her . . .

He could have been behind the calls all along. He kept you away from the media, away from anyone who might have really helped you.

She couldn't have been fooled by him this badly.

But he'd stood there and watched Forster present the report. His report. Publicly condemning you. With you conveniently hours away, where you could do nothing.

Her heart's cries were slowly extinguished by the greater, more insidious force of doubt. What more proof did she need?

The Predator.

She quickly yanked on her clothes, and walked into the kitchen. She lifted the phone, dialed directory assistance. "I want the number for the *Washington Post* please, Metro Section."

When she reached the *Post*, she said, "Sarah Greene, please."

"What in the hell do you mean she's not there?" He tightened his grip on the phone against the overpowering need to send it straight into the nearest wall. "Where did she go?"

"I don't know," Jarrett responded. "I took Wolfman out, then stopped in Rae's shop on my way back to the house."

"How did she get off the mountain?"

"She took Rae's Jeep."

"She what?" Why would she do something like that? Then a sickening thought occurred to him. No, she couldn't have heard. . . . Oh God.

"Dane, listen, I'm—"

"Was the television on when you came back in? Or the radio? Anywhere she might have heard the news?"

"Yeah, in the bathroom. I searched the house immediately when I saw Rae's truck gone. She took a bath or something just before she left. The radio was still on in the bathroom."

Dane swore. She'd heard Forster's little surprise speech. And Dane knew just how damning that must have sounded. She'd moved fast; the broadcast had been less than an hour before. And it had been a very eventful hour.

"Tell me where you want me and I'm there," Jarrett said.

"No, thanks. You did more than enough. It's not your fault." Dane paused, half-afraid to ask the next question, but knowing he had to. "Did she leave any kind of message?"

"Not intentionally. But she did use the phone and scribble the number on the pad next to it. I found it in the trash."

"Who does it connect to?" he asked.

"The *Washington Post*."

It was worse than Dane had thought. She hadn't even been willing to talk to him first. If Adria got to the press before he got to her, everything he'd spent the last hour achieving would go straight to hell. And Adria would be in more than a little danger.

"Connect with Beaudine for me. Tell her I've got it under control and don't need her to keep looking. Thank her for me. I'll explain it all to both of you later." Right now he had to figure out how to play the situation with Adria.

"Sure thing. Is there anything else I can do?"

That's when Dane realized exactly what he was going to do. "You still got that *Post* number handy?"

TWELVE

Adria pushed the truck to the limit. "Why in the hell does Jarrett have to live so far out in the boonies?" she grumbled for the millionth time since leaving the mountain cabin.

Hurt and betrayal began to creep in on the anger again. The tears she refused to shed stung her eyes.

"Damn him," she whispered raggedly. She was such an idiot! She'd been lying there in the tub, fantasizing about having his baby. God, how humiliating. She sniffed and frowned hard, trying to stop the renewed threat of tears.

A car pulled out from a side road and zoomed in right behind her, almost on her bumper. She hit an open stretch of remote country highway and slowed down a bit, hoping the jerk would pass her. He didn't. He got alongside of her and hung there. She slowed down some more, but he also slowed. Irritated, she tried to see into the small gray sedan. "What the hell—"

Dane.

Instead of lifting her foot off the pedal, she floored it. They were coming to another incline, but Dane didn't back off or pass her. He stayed right beside her.

A truck was coming toward them, barreling down the incline. Directly toward Dane. The truck was applying its brakes; she could see the smoke from the tires. The driver was blowing his horn.

Adria had no idea what sort of game Dane was playing now, but she wasn't going to be a party to it. The solution was simple. She pulled off the road, slamming to a complete stop.

Dane immediately pulled into her lane, then swerved to a halt off the road fifty yards in front of her. The trucker barreled by, blaring his horn and giving Dane the finger.

Adria was breathing hard, but thinking very clearly. Perhaps more clearly than she had since she'd heard Forster's statement.

She looked up and saw Dane fling open his car door, climb out, and begin stalking back toward her. Adrenaline was drilling through her veins and she relished the feeling. It gave her the strength to do what had to be done. If

Dane Colbourne wanted a showdown, she'd give him one he'd never forget.

With deliberate calm, she opened the truck door and slid her feet to the gravel-strewn roadside. She closed the door, leaned against it, casually crossing one foot over the other.

As Dane closed the distance between them with long, ground-chewing steps, she realized two things. He was furious.

And he'd finally lost his inimitable control.

It should have scared her. It didn't. It thrilled her, excited her. Made her feel more alive, more a participant in life, than she'd ever felt.

She'd planned to let him get about ten feet away before speaking, but her nerves were badly frayed and it took her a few seconds to make certain her voice would be level and emotionless when she spoke.

He was within touching distance now, and when she looked straight into his eyes, what she found there wasn't unmitigated fury. No, the green-and-gold eyes were filled with hurt.

How dare he hurt, she thought furiously, more than a bit confused. *I'm* the one who got hurt here. But her knees began to shake.

He stopped less than a foot away from her, breathing hard. His hair was windblown, his jaw unshaven. His tie was gone and his jacket forgotten. His sleeves were rolled up and the collar wilted.

Where was the Predator, the man who had coldheartedly manipulated her? This Dane Colbourne looked fierce and vulnerable, fatigued and energized.

Her fingers dug into her palm, the pain there a welcome diversion from the pain in her heart. She'd had no idea of how ripped up she'd feel upon seeing him again.

"I loved you." She flung it between them as an accusation.

"You sure as hell have an odd way of showing it."

"I heard your press conference," she said. "Congratulations on filing your report on time. Guess the system always wins."

He said nothing. Simply stared at her for a long, very uncomfortable while. Adria spent her last bit of control facing him directly, letting him see that she would not be broken, not be devastated by what he'd done to her.

But when the last bit of energy drained from her, leaving her hollow and empty, he still stared at her, relentlessly holding her gaze, daring her to look away.

Daring her to let him see her truth.

As he was letting her see his.

But his truth confused her. His hurt, his anger.

"Did you really think I wouldn't find out?" she demanded. "That you could just keep me tucked away until it was all over? Did you really expect me to take this lying down?"

"Get in the car," he ordered. The mask was firmly back in place. It shone in his eyes, in his face, in his posture.

"Why should I? I can't just—"

"You've proven quite effectively you '*can just*' whenever you see fit. Now it's my turn." He turned and walked away. Knowing she'd follow.

Only when they were back on the road did she attempt to speak. "Am I allowed to ask where we're going?"

"You have an appointment to keep," he answered.

She didn't waste time questioning how he'd found out. "It won't do you any good to try to stop me," she announced.

"I have no intentions of stopping you."

"I've already told her about the third plane," she lied.

"I know exactly what you told Ms. Greene. I spoke to her shortly after you did."

Was he being honest? She couldn't tell a damn thing from his blank expression. "Then why take me to her? I'm certain the last thing you want right now is for me to discuss my theory about that third plane."

He suddenly swerved the car off the road and shut the engine off. He turned to her, his face no longer expressionless, the intensity of emotion in his voice unparalleled. "You don't have any idea about what I want."

Startled, she spoke without thinking. "Until a few hours ago I thought you wanted me."

For a split second his eyes looked bleak. "So did I," he said. Then he did something totally unexpected. He turned away from her. He sat there, silent, staring through the windshield to the empty roadway ahead.

Adria couldn't recall a single time when Dane hadn't faced her down, no matter the circumstance—or consequence. He might hide behind his emotionless mask, but he never hid completely.

And then the truth struck her. His emotionless mask hadn't been a mask at all. He'd actually closed down, locked away all his feelings, relying only on sharp instinct and dogged determination to deal with life. Which in his case was his career. A career that revolved around finding out why planes collided, crashed, or blew up. Usually, if not always, taking innocent lives with them.

How could anybody cope with such violence? Exactly as Dane had. By shutting down.

Shame and embarrassment flooded Adria. For her, he'd let down his walls, compromised his integrity, and put his faith in her when every piece of evidence pointed otherwise.

And how had she repaid him?

Shaking, she reached out, knowing he was

well within his rights to pull away from her touch. She covered the hand tightly gripping the steering wheel with her own. He didn't flinch.

Somehow that was worse. As if she didn't matter at all.

"Dane, please look at me." When he made no move other than to tighten his jaw, she took a breath and added, "I need to say some things to you and I think it serves me right to have to look you in the eyes when I say them."

He released the steering wheel and slid his hand from under hers. But she persisted.

"Please," she whispered. "I know I hurt you. Please let me apologize. Whatever you want to do after that is up to you."

He turned to face her. She'd expected his shields to be up and doubled in strength. Instead she found him open, all the way to his soul. No protection. His pain, his anger, his dashed hopes—all were laid bare for her to see. The enormity of what he had given her—of what she'd so hastily tossed back in his face—hit her with a force that literally shook her.

"Dear God," she whispered. "What have I done?" Eyes burning, voice shaking, she lifted a badly trembling hand toward him, but couldn't quite touch him. She wondered if she'd ever truly touch him again. "I was so busy protecting myself," she began hoarsely.

"So busy making sure no one ever took advantage of me again. No," she said, ruthlessly digging deeper. "That's not really true. I was trying to make sure I didn't *allow* anyone to take advantage of me. And then the incident happened." She let her hand drop lifelessly to the seat between them, then slowly curled it into a fist. "I was scared. Scared that I'd lose the one thing I had control over—my career. I had made the mistake of thinking that control extended to my whole life." She laughed, but it was a hollow, bitter sound. "Then you came along. I got to know you, to want you—" She took a shaky breath when heat flared in his eyes, almost, but not quite, vanquishing the bleakness and anger. Still, it gave her strength to go on. "And I realized I was fooling myself. I had no life. Just a career."

She swallowed and tried to control the wavering note in her voice that threatened to make it impossible to speak at all. "But even when the evidence piled up against me, you had faith in me. You . . . wanted me. *Me.* And I began to fall in love with you." Tears burned their way past her eyelids and trickled down her face. "I did fall in love with you. Do you know how frightening it was to realize how much I counted on having you there for me? How badly I needed to lean on you? It was such a huge risk for me, I couldn't see past it. Couldn't see what you had risked to believe me, to let yourself care for me, or what you had to overcome to give so much of yourself to me." She pulled her hand into her lap and clutched at it with her other. He sat there, unblinking, unmoved.

"But worst of all," she continued, knowing she had to say it all, for both of their sakes. "After all that has happened between us, all that you have taken from me on faith when I knew you've found your security in life relying only on fact . . . The first time it appears that you used me, might have had ulterior motives for what we'd done together, I panicked and ran. I assumed I'd let myself be duped again, and I felt righteously angry and betrayed."

Her voice dropped to the merest whisper. "When all the time, the only person being betrayed was you. Your trust. Your faith. And for that, I don't think I'll ever forgive myself. And I understand that you won't—shouldn't—either. But I'm sorry. It doesn't make it right, and God knows I've never been more ashamed of myself, but I'm sorry I doubted you."

She lapsed into silence, feeling emptier than she could ever recall feeling. Not even when her father had died. No longer able to look at Dane, she dropped her gaze to her tangled fingers.

They sat there like that for a while. Adria counted each heartbeat. It seemed to mock her. How could life continue when she felt so dead inside?

"Of all the people in the world, I can understand the need for proof. For solid evidence."

Adria looked up, startled to hear him speak.

"Perhaps I didn't give you the kind of solid proof you needed. Maybe it's been as . . . scary for me as it has been for you."

"Dane—"

He cut her off with a gesture of his hand. "When I heard from Jarrett that you'd left," he went on, "I was angry that you'd doubted me, but my first instinct was to come after you to give you evidence. To prove to you that I wouldn't betray you."

"And now?" Adria forced herself to ask, knowing she deserved the pain of his certain answer.

"Don't you want to know what I found out? Isn't that the only important thing left?"

"No," she said instantly. "I meant what I said, Dane. I don't need to hear."

"Yes, you do. *I* need you to hear." His gaze challenged her to interrupt as he went on to explain about the foreign coating.

"Eliot had a hunch that it might be military. With Forster's apparent involvement, I figured air force. Then I immediately thought Stealth plane. If they were testing something like a surveillance plane in the area that night, they certainly wouldn't want anyone to know about it. So what if this plane happened to wander in to your airspace by accident? Maybe it didn't cloak itself from radar detection until the pilot was alerted to his mistake? That would explain why it appeared in your display from out of nowhere. And then it gets involved in a midair collision that could have ended up in a huge ball of fire if not for the quick thinking of an air-traffic controller and some fancy maneuvering by two very well-trained pilots. Three if you count the military-plane pilot."

"What about the ARTS tapes? It should have been on there."

Dane shook his head. "I hadn't figured that part out when I heard about the news conference. I didn't have time to contact you. And when I got to the conference, Forster was careful not to let me speak. But I cornered him afterward. I knew enough, had pieced together enough, that I was certain I could bluff him."

"What did he do?"

"He made a deal. No way was he going to chance me going to the press, or worse, someone higher up than him."

"Didn't he realize you'd flip when you heard about his announcement? He'd turned in a falsified report with your name on it!"

"At that point he pretty well figured he

had me over a barrel because of my personal involvement with you."

"He knew?" Then she put it all together. "The military got to him after the incident. Convinced him to help cover it up."

Dane nodded. "I'd already been put on the case by the time they got to Forster. After the preliminary report, it was obvious to him that you would be the easy fall guy. You'd had two reprimands recently, both taken without defense or protest. He figured with some pressure on me about another case I was on, I'd get this one in. He didn't count on you pushing your third-plane scenario despite the lack of evidence in the ARTS tapes."

"How did that happen?"

"The military immediately had someone back into the computer and erase the data."

Adria couldn't have been more astonished. "Boy, that third plane must be very high up on the security ladder."

Dane nodded.

"So, Forster was behind the calls?" Adria asked. "The fake reporter?"

Dane nodded again. "When it became obvious to him that neither of us was going to let the case drop easily, he got another intelligence officer to contact you in the guise of a reporter, to check up on exactly what you were talking about and to whom. The first warning call was to keep you from contacting Sarah Greene at the *Post*."

"Thereby blowing her cover."

"Right. But when you kept seeing me and I kept stalling for time, they pressed harder. On both of us. They had no idea that I was there that last time. They thought by dropping my name, you'd back off for good."

Adria shook her head, boggled by what had really been going on, but even more boggled by the fact that it actually made sense. "How did you find out all this?"

"I had an ace in the hole. I'd had Eliot send a second piece of fuselage with the paint on it to the metallurgy lab. I started bluffing Forster with what I had put together so far, and when I realized how nervous I was making him, I took the risk of telling him I already knew what was on the fuselage. I told him Eliot or the lab would find out shortly if we didn't cut some sort of deal."

"Which was?"

"That he tell me everything. And that you be exonerated."

"He couldn't have had the clearance to do that."

"Time was of the essence. You'd be surprised how swiftly things can be declassified when national security is at stake. I was ushered into the air-force offices in fifteen minutes, and less than thirty minutes later I had the whole story."

"What happens to the information now?" Adria asked. "The report has been filed."

"The unofficial records will be sealed. Officially, the FAA will rule that your negligence couldn't be proven to their satisfaction. You'll receive a documented reprimand for the TCAS you overrode, but otherwise it will be over. I had to sign a statement prohibiting me from discussing this matter with anyone. Ever. You were to come in for the same debriefing and signature. That's when I called you."

"And I was gone." Adria's mind returned instantly to the fact that while, in the end, she'd kept her job, she'd ultimately lost the only real thing of value. Dane.

"So that's why you came after me?" she asked. "To get me to the debriefing and sign the statement?"

"I knew from Jarrett that you'd called the *Post*. I had to stop you before you talked to Sarah Greene."

"Is that the only reason?" It almost killed her to ask, but she hadn't been able to stop herself.

Dane looked away for a brief moment, then back at her. His expression shuttered. "Halfway here I changed my mind. I knew that what you planned to do would ruin everything, but at that point I had stopped thinking like an investigator. That was when I got angry." His gaze was heated, but not with passion.

Adria fought the urge not to shiver.

"I got angry like I haven't been since I found out my father had died. And it's a useless, unproductive, exhausting emotion, that sort of anger. I learned that lesson the hard way as a kid. But this time I couldn't seem to stop it," he said quietly. "Or control it, harness it and turn it around and make it work for me. Like I've been doing for most of my life."

Adria didn't know what to do. She felt her insides winding into a knot of despair. She hated that she had brought him to this. "I'm so sorry," she said. "It sounds so stupid and clichéd, but I never meant to hurt you."

"I actually stopped, was ready to turn around," he said, as if she'd never spoken. "At that moment I really didn't care if you jeopardized everything by running to the media or that you might be putting yourself in more danger than you could comprehend because you didn't know all the facts. I told myself that I didn't care if my career was ruined either. After all, it was my own stupid fault for breaking every rule I'd ever set, crossing the lines I'd drawn years ago for good reasons."

"So why did you come? Why did you stop me?"

The anger fled from his eyes, leaving only pain.

"Because I love you."

Adria gasped, choking on her grief for what she'd done.

"And I can't stop just because you're running off to do something stupid that hurts me. I can't stop just because you thought I could actually intentionally hurt you. I can't stop just because it's easier to give up, easier to crawl back into my hole, easier to shut myself off again. I can't stop." He cleared his throat, but his beautiful eyes burned as his gaze bore into hers. "Because I want you. I want what I know damn well we can have. And now that you've dragged me into it, I'm not giving it, or you, up without a fight."

Her tears were flowing hotter and heavier now. "I don't deserve it. Or you. But I'd be worse than a liar if I said I don't want that, too. No matter what." She reached over and took his hand, twining her fingers with his. "Because I do love you. I don't know, maybe that's why I was so quick to run. You're intense and so focused and always in control. You scare the hell out of me. I wish, desperately, that I had been as brave with my love as you have." She broke off, then choking down a sob, she said, "But I've never loved anyone like I love you. I won't ever run away from that again."

"Then I say maybe we do deserve each other," he said. "Maybe we exactly deserve each other."

Adria clung on to his hand, and to the hope she saw in his eyes, like a lifeline.

He tugged her closer, then lifted a hand to her neck. She released a long, trembling sigh. "You feel so good," she said.

"You forced me to feel again, Adria. It scares me, but I don't want to stop. I want more, a whole lot more. I want to explore it all. With you there dragging me along kicking and screaming."

The tiniest of smiles curved her lips. "Kicking and screaming?" She sniffed, then laughed. "You? I don't think so. You're big and tough and like a steamroller, so I guess it'll be a challenge not to let you just roll over me." Her smile broadened as the last of the pain left his eyes, to be replaced by slow, deep heat. "I want that challenge, I need it." She lifted her hand to the back of his neck and tugged him closer, delighting in the fact that he came willingly. "I need you."

Just before his lips touched hers, he said, "You got me. Forever, if you want me."

"I do."

Dane pulled back slightly and let a slow, wide smile crease his face. When she gasped, he knew he'd just found his purpose for the rest of his life.

"How about I put that white tuxedo back on and you say that again."

Pleasure and hope and a love so bright he wondered that he'd been lucky enough to find it shone on her face. A trace of devilry crept into her expression and Dane felt his entire body harden. Yes, he'd found his purpose all right.

And he was just as certain she'd found hers when she said, "I think I'd rather see you in something like jeans and a T-shirt. A real tight T-shirt. The jeans too."

"What are the chances that you'll ever react like I expect you to?" he asked, but he was already lowering his mouth back to hers. "Never mind," he whispered against her lips. "Surprise me."

And she did.

And he thanked God for it, and her, and would every day for the rest of his life.

EPILOGUE

Dane leaned back on the railing of the porch that wrapped around the front and side of Zach's big farmhouse. His wife of one month was nestled with her back against his chest; his arms were wrapped comfortably around her waist. He was surrounded by those closest to him. He couldn't remember ever feeling so content.

"Strange about Forster resigning like that," Zach said casually. He was lounging on the porch swing, Dara snuggled up against him.

Adria glanced up at Dane, but neither gave anything away. Dane merely shrugged.

"At least Adria was cleared in the final report," Dara put in.

Dane smiled, both in response to his sister's comment and because he was pleased that

Adria had hit it off well with his sister. In fact, she'd fit in seamlessly with all of them.

"Any word on who's replacing him?" Jarrett asked.

"You mean you didn't hear?" Adria responded. She kissed Dane, who had to endure Zach's whoop and Jarrett's approving smile. "Dane's up for his job."

Zach pumped his fist in the air and laid a hard kiss on Dara's mouth.

Dara laughed. "What was that for?"

"Just celebrating family success the only way I know how, sweetheart." Dara didn't flush at all; she just tucked Zach's hand more tightly around her shoulders, then whispered something in his ear.

Rae suddenly cleared her throat, drawing everyone's attention. "Congratulations, Dane," she said, her smile wide and sincere. "I know you'll get the job." She glanced up at Jarrett for a moment, as if seeking approval.

"You want to tell them?" he asked her. She held his gaze for a moment, then Jarrett turned back to his now avid audience.

With a dull flush staining his neck, Jarrett reached into his back pocket and pulled out a folded piece of paper. "We have some news of our own."

He unfolded the paper, stared down at it, then looked up, his pleasure a palpable thing. He pulled Rae against him and let his hand fall on her stomach. "We wanted to wait awhile, until things were further along." He stumbled to a halt, then simply said, "We're going to have a baby."

Everyone immediately erupted into shouts of congratulations, which woke Wolfman from his sleeping place in a patch of sun at the top of the stairs. He barked and circled the group as they hovered around Rae and Jarrett to look at the sonogram picture of the fetus that was on the paper.

When hugs and kisses had been exchanged and all the details had been discussed, things settled down and a peaceful quiet stole over the group.

"You know," Dane said after a long, comfortable silence, "I never thought we'd all be back here." He hugged Adria. "Like this."

"Pretty great, isn't it?" Zach said. He smiled down at Dara. "When can we make one of those funny little pictures?"

Her only answer was a knowing smile.

"So," Zach said, his eyes twinkling with mischief, "we all agree we're disgustingly happy. I say we spread the joy." He waggled his eyebrows. "Who's next?"

Beaudine chose that exact moment to walk out onto the porch. "What's all this racket about out here? Am I the only one who gets any work done around here anymore?" She shook her head, then stilled when she realized six heads had turned her way.

"What trouble you all cookin' up now?" Her threatening tone was at odds with the wary expression creeping into her eyes.

As if on cue, Zach, Dane, and Jarrett looked at one another, then at Beaudine.

Beaudine took a step backward. "Don't you go staring like that at me." She shook her finger at them. "You got wives now. You're all family men."

Zach grabbed Dara's hand and leaned away from the post. "Come now, *chère*." He prodded Beaudine in a dead-on imitation. "We just want you to be as happy as we are, *ma petite*." Dane, Adria, Jarrett, and Rae all moved to stand beside them. "Don't you think it's about time you put ol' Frank out of his misery?"

Before Beaudine could say a word, Zach turned and put his hand out, palm down, in the center of the circle. Dara's hand closed over his, immediately followed by Jarrett, Rae, then Dane, and finally Adria.

"I'll call Frank," Dara said.

"I'll call the preacher," Rae chimed in.

"I'll take care of the clothes," Adria put in.

"I'll give away the bride," Zach declared.

"I can pull some strings on a license," Jarrett said.

"You don't think she's had a license since

the day Frank caught the bouquet at my wedding?" Zach asked.

Jarrett nodded. "I guess I could handle being best man."

Dane looked at each one of them, then said, "All for one?"

"And one for all," the rest intoned simultaneously.

They lifted their still-joined hands above their heads, then broke apart, turning as one toward Beaudine.

"*Merde,*" she whispered under her breath.

When they advanced toward her, she swore in Cajun. Then took off with a shriek into the house.

The ceremony took place that evening. It was lovely, if unorthodox.

The bride wore red, the groom wore a smile.

And everyone rejoiced.

The Three Musketeers had returned to Madison County.

THE

Loveswept

EDITORS
ARE HAPPY TO ANNOUNCE
THE THREE WINNERS OF
LOVESWEPT'S TREASURED
TALES III CONTEST!

**THERESA BURCHETT
CHRISTY M. ANDERSON
LESLIE-ANN JONES**

OUR CONGRATULATIONS TO
EACH OF THESE TERRIFIC AND
LOYAL LOVESWEPT FANS. TO
READ THEIR PROFILES, PLEASE
TURN THE PAGE.

AND MANY THANKS TO
EVERYONE WHO ENTERED THE
CONTEST.

Theresa Burchett

Theresa is from Southern California, where she has lived all of her life. She is married and is the proud mother of a son and a daughter. Reading is without question a passion of Theresa's—she usually reads a book a day! She has been reading romance for fifteen years, and says that Loveswept is her favorite series because the stories and characters are always interesting. "Years after reading one of your books I could pick it up and remember the characters. Like old friends, they stay in my thoughts," she says.

Theresa's favorite authors include Tami Hoag, Deborah Smith, Sandra Brown, Billie Green, Kay Hooper, Sandra Chastain, and most of all, Iris Johansen.

Christy M. Anderson

Christy got married recently, the day before she mailed her entry to our Treasured Tales III Contest, in fact. Just goes to show that true love can bring good luck as well! Christy is store manager for a men's clothing store as well as an aspiring writer. In her spare time, she likes to work out, loves antiques (especially rings), and of course, loves to read. Christy says that she has been reading romance "since my mother would let me," and her favorite Loveswept authors are Iris Johansen, Jan Hudson, and Fayrene Preston.

Leslie-ann Jones

Leslie-ann was excited to hear that she had won because she says she always enters contests, but never wins. She is a native of Trinidad, and migrated to America with her younger sister to join her mother in 1984. Along with reading (she has 1,327 books, 598 of which are Loveswepts!), Leslie-ann loves sports, animals, collecting stamps, and participating in Carnival. She is also a graduate of Coppin State College, where she earned a B.S. in management science with a minor in computer science.

THE EDITORS' CORNER

What do a cunning cat-burglar, a self-starting sister, a determined detective and a witty workaholic have in common? Nothing but the most romantic of troubles, as you'll find out in next month's LOVE-SWEPTs. So join these four intriguing heroines as they journey the bumpy road to happily-ever-after . . . and discover that love does indeed conquer all.

Romance star Fayrene Preston adds her own brand of heat with the next book in the Damaron Dynasty series: LOVESWEPT #778, **THE DAMARON MARK: THE WARRIOR.** Jonah Damaron exudes power like a force of nature, untamable and sensual in a way that awakens every nerve ending in Jolie Lanier's body! But she's playing a dangerous game, taking risks for the sake of honor, keeping secrets that Jonah's smile promises he can uncover with the merest whisper of a touch. As fast-paced as a lover's heartbeat, as white-hot as the heat of a candle flame, Fayrene Preston's novel blends daring intrigue and desperate passions, joining an irresistible hero and an unforgettable heroine in a timeless tango of love.

No one touches the heart and tickles the funny bone all at once like Marcia Evanick in **FAMILY FIRST**, LOVESWEPT #779. James Stonewall Carson doesn't look like a grade-school teacher, with his muscled body and shoulders broad enough to carry the world. But there's no mistaking his dedication to the job—or his manly interest in Emmy Lou Mc-Nally. Raising six brothers and sisters leaves her no time for dating, but James's sweet talk and fast moves, along with a little help from matchmaking townfolks, pave the way for a delightful courtship. This top-notch read from award-winner Marcia Evanick reveals how tender passion can burn with sizzling heat.

Excitement ripples **UNDER THE COVERS** in Linda Warren's newest LOVESWEPT, #780. He's never been followed by a woman so downright determined, Simon Faro notes with admiration—and more than a touch of curiosity! Detective Jo O'Neal is outrageously persistent in tracking him, even taking on a sassy charade in hopes he'll lead her to criminals she's long been after. Once he proves he's just a reporter nosing around for a scoop, he must convince her to join forces to smoke out the bad guys and set off some fireworks of their own. Linda Warren's steamy romp is a seriously sexy caper that's undeniably fun.

Surrender to the temptation of **SLOW HANDS**, LOVESWEPT #781, by Debra Dixon. Sam Tucker isn't the kind of man to wait for an invitation, not when his mission is to help Clare McGuire learn the joys of losing control! Convinced Sam wants only to change her, the pretty business exec insists she likes her life just as it is—until his kisses brand her with fiery need that echoes her own hunger. Sparring has never been so sweetly seductive as in this delicious treat from Debra Dixon, who entangles a savvy work-aholic with a formerly buttoned-down and bottled-up hero determined to show her how to seize the moment.

Happy reading!

With warmest wishes,

Beth de Guzman

Shauna Summers

Beth de Guzman   Shauna Summers

Senior Editor   Associate Editor

P.S. Watch for these Bantam women's fiction titles coming in February: Tami Hoag's impressive debut hardcover, NIGHT SINS, revealed her to be a masterful spinner of spine-chilling thrills; now, in **GUILTY AS SIN,** she picks up where she left off, delivering non-stop suspense that brings terror to a whole new, even more frightening level. From Teresa Medeiros, nationally bestselling author of FAIREST

OF THEM ALL, comes **BREATH OF MAGIC**, a bewitching time-travel romance about an enchantress from the 17th century who collides with a future beyond her imagining. Finally Jean Stone's **IVY SECRETS** is the emotionally charged story of three former college roommates brought together by the kidnapping of one of their daughters. Be sure to see next month's LOVESWEPTs for a preview of these exceptional novels. And immediately following this page, preview the Bantam women's fiction titles on sale *now*!

Don't miss these extraordinary books
by your favorite Bantam authors

On sale in January:

LION'S BRIDE
by Iris Johansen

SEE HOW THEY RUN
by Bethany Campbell

SCOUNDREL
by Elizabeth Elliott

LION'S BRIDE

BY

IRIS JOHANSEN

A magical weaver of spellbinding tales, enticing characters, and unforgettable romance, Iris Johansen is a "master among master storytellers."* Now the winner of every major romance award returns with a sizzling new novel of passion, peril, and searing sensuality.

The darkly handsome warrior found her in the hot desert night, the last survivor of a caravan devastated by a brutal attack. But Thea could hardly have found a less likely savior. Brooding, powerful, erotic, the infamous Lord Ware felt no need to rescue a total stranger, but Thea's striking beauty and fighting spirit moved him. So the knight in tarnished armor carried her away to his secret stronghold at Dundragon, where she would become his prisoner, his tormentor, his lover . . . and the one weapon his deadly enemy could use to destroy him.

* *Affaire de Coeur*

*From the nationally bestselling master of
romantic suspense*

Bethany Campbell
SEE HOW
THEY RUN

*"Bethany Campbell weaves strong magic
so powerful that it encircles the reader."*
—Romantic Times

*Two innocent autistic children. A beautiful teacher.
A hardened ex-cop.
What they know could get them killed. . . .*

"You can set your watch by him," one of the teachers had said.

That's exactly what the twins did every weekday afternoon on the playground. The boys were eight and very handsome. They had dark hair and blue-gray eyes fringed with black lashes. They wore identical military watches, large and unbreakable.

Each day when the tall old gentleman appeared, rounding the corner, the boys' eyes glittered with interest. They would look first at their watches, then at each other. The watches should say 2:07, and if they did not, the twins adjusted them, because the old man *always* appeared at 2:07.

Laura would be grateful to see the old gentleman round the corner, for that meant recess was almost half over, and soon she would be back in the warmth of the classroom.

The twins, as usual, clutched the fence rails, ignoring the other children, watching for the man. Their winter jackets and gloves were alike in all but color. As usual, Trace wore blue and Rickie red. The boys were so identical that many people could tell them apart only by this color coding. They seemed even to breathe in unison, their breath rising in synchronized plumes toward the sky.

Their hands tightened on the fence when they saw the man coming. The air was so cold that his ears were red and his usually controlled face looked almost pained. His white muffler was wound around his neck, and his coat collar was turned up. He seemed to exhale smoke as he walked, as if he were an elderly and benign dragon.

Perhaps because of the cold, he walked a bit more swiftly than usual, and Trace frowned, trying to keep count of the man's steps. When the old man passed the boys, he lifted his hat, just barely.

"*Good* afternoon," he said, not looking at them, striding on. "*Good* afternoon."

They saluted stiffly, their eyes following him. "*Good* afternoon," they echoed. "*Good* afternoon."

He kept moving briskly. One of the other children, Janine, ran up to Laura, asking for help in retying her shoe. "Of course," Laura said, putting her hand on the girl's shoulder. But she waited, first, to exchange her usual silent greeting with the old gentleman.

His dark eyes met hers. He raised his gloved hand to his hat. He nodded.

Then a long staccato burst of noise split the winter air, and the side of the old gentleman's face exploded into blood. His remaining eye rolled upward, his shattered jaw fell, as if to cry out, but no sound emerged.

Blood blossomed on his chest like red carnations sprouting in full bloom, and blood spurted from his legs, which danced, sinking beneath him. He lurched like a broken puppet toward the street and fell in a ruined heap. His wounds steamed like little mouths exhaling into the cold.

The children screamed, the teachers on the playground screamed, pedestrians screamed, and one woman with a Lord & Taylor shopping bag sat on the sidewalk, screaming as blood poured down her face.

Laura moved on sheer instinct. She wrestled Janine to the ground before the old gentleman hit the sidewalk, and she held her there, her body thrown over the girl's. *Shooting*, Laura thought in horror, ducking her head, *somebody's shooting at us*.

A bullet richocheted shrilly off the pavement of the playground, and one of the children—William, perhaps?—screamed even more loudly.

Her face hidden, she heard Herschel's agonized cry. "He's hit! He's hit!"

Then the shooting stopped and she heard the squeal of tires. Without the shots, the air seemed to ring with silence—except for the screams, of course, but they hardly registered on Laura's consciousness any longer.

"He's hit! He's hit!" Herschel's voice was broken. She looked over her shoulder, biting her lip. Herschel knelt above William, who flailed and writhed, holding his arm.

The other children were crying as teachers tried to drag them back inside the safety of the school.

Numbly Laura clutched the sobbing Janine closer to her chest. She forced herself to look at the old gentleman again. He lay motionless on the sidewalk in the welter of his blood.

His beautiful overcoat is ruined, she thought illogically. And just as illogically, a line from *Macbeth* ran through her head: *"Who'd have thought the old man to have so much blood in him?"*

So much blood.

Then, with a shock, she realized that Trace and Rickie still hung onto the fence as if hypnotized, staring at the corpse. They alone of all the children were not crying or shrieking.

They regarded the dead man, the dark pool of blood, the screaming wounded woman, with wooden faces. Their hands still gripped the fence bars, and a slow, thin stream of scarlet ran down Trace's cheek, dropping to stain the bright blue of his coat.

Oh, God, he's shot, Laura thought in panic. She rose and stumbled to the boys although Janine screamed out for her to stay.

Quickly she examined Trace's cheek. It bled profusely, but he didn't seem to notice. He acted irritated that she had pulled him away from the fence.

Janine got to her feet and lurched toward Laura, hysterical. She grasped her around the waist and wouldn't let go. "Shh, shh," Laura told the girl, her voice shaking. "We'll go inside. We'll be fine inside."

Rickie, too, was annoyed to be pulled away from

the fence rails and clung to them more tightly. "Shots," he said. "Shots. The man got shooted on the hundred-and-twenty-ninth step."

"Yes, yes," she said impatiently, wrenching him from the fence. She was terrified that whoever had opened fire would return and shoot again.

She wrapped on arm around the bleeding Trace, the other around Rickie. Janine still hung onto her waist, wailing hysterically.

In the distance, sirens shrilled. "The police are coming," she told the children, struggling to herd them inside. "The police will be here, and we'll be safe."

"The car come by," Rickie said, frowning studiously. "The car shot. Hit the man."

Trace touched his own cheek, then regarded his bloodied glove impassively. He nodded. "The car shot. Hit the man."

A drive-by shooting. Here—in front of our own school, in front of these poor children, Laura thought. *The world's gone crazy. The world's mad.*

Somehow, Laura maneuvered her little brood inside the school.

"I've called nine-one-one," Mrs. Marcuse, the school's director, said, struggling to exert control. "The police will be here. An ambulance will be here." She held up her hands as if beseeching them for peace, but there was none.

Jilly, the oldest student, crouched in a corner, hugging herself, her expression full of terror. She covered her eyes with her hands, as if she could block out what she had witnessed.

Oh, my God, that they should see this—Laura

thought, still in shock—*that children should see such a thing.*

Laura knelt before Trace. She snatched off her muffler and dabbed it against his cheek. "Does it hurt?" she asked.

He ignored her question. He frowned at the door. "Car shot thirty times," he said, jutting his lower lip out petulantly. "Hit the man nineteen. The man didn't finish the walk. Got to finish the walk."

"He can't finish his walk. Trace, look at me. Tell me if you're hit any place else. Do you hurt anywhere else?"

Stolid, he didn't answer. He stared at the door instead, and Laura thought that maybe the wound in his cheek was only superficial. She kept her muffler pressed against it, willing her hand not to shake.

"I saw the license," Rickie said quietly. "It was MPZ one oh four eight one nine."

Trace nodded. "MPZ one oh four eight one nine. The man should finish the walk."

The hall was overwarm, almost stifling, but Laura suddenly went cold. Once more a peculiar silence enclosed her, blocking the riot of sound.

"What?" She clutched Trace's jacket by the lapel. "Say that to me again."

He frowned more irritably. "MPZ one oh four eight one nine. The man should finish the walk."

Her heart beat painfully hard as she turned to Rickie. "You saw the license number?"

"MPZ one oh four eight one nine," he said.

My God, she thought with a rush of adrenaline. *They both got the license number.*

SCOUNDREL

by Elizabeth Elliott
author of THE WARLORD

**In a world of war and intrigue,
the greatest danger of all is in
daring to love. . . .**

Lady Lily Walters played her part to perfection. Her low-cut gowns and empty chatter kept everyone from guessing the truth—that this sensuous flirt was really a spy. Willingly, she risked her life to pass on vital secrets only she could divulge. But when the dangerously attractive Duke of Remmington took her in his arms, she found herself wishing just once she could drop her masquerade and show him the woman that she really was. . . .

"Well, I'm in no hurry to find myself in a state that makes most men I know positively morose. Although I'll admit that—" Harry stopped in midsentence. "Good God. Will you look at that."

Remmington turned around at his friend's insistence. One could see almost anything on the streets of London, but his face registered surprise at the sight that greeted him.

The new gaslights of Saint James's Street revealed the shadowy form of a woman as she raced down the middle of the foggy street, her figure vague and muted in the dim light. He watched with an eerie sense of the surreal as she drew nearer and her features became distinct.

The fog that surrounded her began to drift away, a trick of the eye that made her look as if she emerged from the night itself. The voluminous folds of a dark blue robe billowed out from her waist like silk sails in a brisk wind. The skirt of a pristine white nightgown revealed itself beneath the robe, and her flight outlined long, lithe legs against the smooth fabric. Waist-length auburn hair floated over her shoulders in fiery waves. One slender hand held the skirt of her robe and nightgown above the path of her slippered feet while the other hand clutched her throat. The expression on her face was one of sheer terror. She glanced over her shoulder several times, as though certain the hounds of hell were on her heels.

The girl was less than fifteen feet away when Remmington swore under his breath, recognizing the shadowy figure at last. He thought she was running right to him, but she changed direction at the last moment, obviously intent on the entrance to White's. Two long strides from the side of the carriage and he intercepted her. He caught her with one outstretched arm and her breath came out in a whoosh. He pushed her toward Harry and the waiting carriage.

"Get her inside, man. She can't be seen on the street!" Remmington spun around to face the club's doorman. The liveried servant's mouth hung wide open. He pressed ten pounds into the man's palm. "One word of this incident and I will know where to direct my anger."

Remmington didn't think it possible, but the man's eyes actually opened wider as he stared at the money.

"No! My father!" the girl cried out. She tried to pull away from Harry's grip. Her voice sounded strained, and she put her hand again to the high, ruffled neckline of her nightgown. She turned her attention to Remmington, both hands at her neck now as if she found it painful to speak. "He's . . . inside."

"No, he isn't," Remmington replied.

Harry stared down at the woman in silence, his expression incredulous. "Good God! Lady—"

"Shut up," Remmington snapped. He turned Harry toward the door to his carriage. "Just get her inside before anyone else sees her."

Harry pushed Lady Lillian into the plush carriage and took the seat opposite hers. Remmington followed a moment later, then he signaled to the driver with a rap on the roof before he sat next to Lily. She clutched at his arm as the carriage lurched forward, but pushed away from him as soon as she regained her balance. Her breath came in quick pants and he could feel her tremble. The fear in her eyes made him uneasy.

"Would you mind telling us just what you are doing on the streets at this time of night?"

"Must find . . ." She lifted her hand to her throat. Her words died on a hoarse whisper. ". . . Papa."

He reached out to push aside the lacy frills that concealed her neck. She slapped his hand away, but not quickly enough. The ugly red marks on her throat made him swear under his breath. Someone had tried to strangle her! Rage flowed through him, instant and potent, but he forced his voice to remain calm. "Who did this to you, Lily?"

Harry leaned forward. He'd also noticed the bruises. "Give us the name and we'll take care of the blackguard."

"Don't . . . know. Must . . . find—"

"There, there, Lillian," Harry said. "We'll take you home to Crofford House and get to the bottom of this foul deed." Harry leaned forward to place his hand over hers, but Lily jerked away and pressed herself even further into the corner of the carriage.

"No!" She shook her head.

"We're not going to hurt you," Remmington murmured. "We only want to help you, Lily. Are you afraid that whoever did this is still in your house?"

Her gaze moved slowly to Harry, then back again before she finally nodded. Remmington covered her hand before he remembered that she'd refused the same meager comfort from Harry. He was absurdly pleased when she didn't draw away from him. "How many were there?"

"I saw . . . one," she said with difficulty. "I screamed . . . no one came. Please take—"

"How many servants are in residence?"

"Seven."

Remmington frowned. Not an unusually large number of servants, but enough that one should have heard her cries for help. Harry's comment echoed his thoughts.

"It seems unlikely that just one man could take care of seven servants."

Lily tugged on Remmington's sleeve. "Papa is at White's."

He winced at the sound of her raspy voice, then slowly shook his head. "No, Lily. I saw your father leave White's an hour ago. Where else might he be?"

Her expression grew uncertain. "I don't know."

He exchanged a worried glance with Harry, then nodded toward the trapdoor in the ceiling. "Tell the driver to take us to my house."

Harry stood up to carry out the order, but Lily shook her head. "I cannot—"

"We will stop just long enough to get some of my men," Remmington told her, "then we will all go check on your servants. If your father doesn't turn up in the meantime, I will send someone out to search for him."

She nodded, but her hands were clenched in tight fists, her lower lip caught between her teeth. There was a look of bewildered fear in her eyes. As he gazed down at her stricken face, he was nearly overwhelmed by the need to take her into his arms and keep her safe. He wanted to kill the man who did this to her.

"Can you describe the man who attacked you?" His frustration deepened when she shook her head. "Can you remember anything at all? The color of his eyes? His height or size? Are you certain it was not a servant, or someone you know?"

Her breaths became more rapid and shallow with each question. She held one hand to her throat, the other to her forehead.

"Take a deep breath," he ordered, worried she would faint. He knew from his experience in battles that anyone frightened this badly would respond more readily to command than to pity. "That's right. Now take one more and you'll feel better."

She took several before her breathing returned to a more normal rate. "Too many . . . questions. No answers."

He didn't quite believe her. She had to remember something. She must be too shaken to recall the answers clearly at the moment, but he didn't know how to calm her down.

"We need a plan. Give me a moment to think this through." Unable to concentrate when he looked at her, he pushed aside the carriage curtains and gazed out at the night. He closed his eyes and pictured the marks that lined her throat. By tomorrow, they would be dark, vicious bruises. He couldn't imagine that any sane man would take that slender throat between his hands to deliberately choke the life from her. He could think of any number of things a man might want to do to a beautiful, defenseless woman, but murder was not one of them.

His hands became fists as he wondered just what sort of man she'd encountered. Perhaps she'd stumbled across a common thief, startled him enough that he'd turned on her. Only a fool would rob a house when the family was in residence, yet who else would try to kill her? It was a daring plan, but a definite possibility. If a thief knew that Lily and her father were at a ball, it would be logical to assume they would remain there until the very early hours of the morning. Yet that night Lily had gone home early, and Remmington knew the reason why.

His gaze returned to her. If he hadn't interfered in her life earlier that evening, she might still be at the Ashlands' ball. Without thinking, he reached out to stroke her cheek. "Don't worry, Lily. You're safe now."

On sale in February:

GUILTY AS SIN
by Tami Hoag

BREATH OF MAGIC
by Teresa Medeiros

IVY SECRETS
by Jean Stone

To enter the sweepstakes outlined below, you must respond by the date specified and follow all entry instructions published elsewhere in this offer.

DREAM COME TRUE SWEEPSTAKES

Sweepstakes begins 9/1/94, ends 1/15/96. To qualify for the Early Bird Prize, entry must be received by the date specified elsewhere in this offer. Winners will be selected in random drawings on 2/29/96 by an independent judging organization whose decisions are final. Early Bird winner will be selected in a separate drawing from among all qualifying entries.

Odds of winning determined by total number of entries received. Distribution not to exceed 300 million.

Estimated maximum retail value of prizes: Grand (1) $25,000 (cash alternative $20,000); First (1) $2,000; Second (1) $750; Third (50) $75; Fourth (1,000) $50; Early Bird (1) $5,000. Total prize value: $86,500.

Automobile and travel trailer must be picked up at a local dealer; all other merchandise prizes will be shipped to winners. Awarding of any prize to a minor will require written permission of parent/guardian. If a trip prize is won by a minor, s/he must be accompanied by parent/legal guardian. Trip prizes subject to availability and must be completed within 12 months of date awarded. Blackout dates may apply. Early Bird trip is on a space available basis and does not include port charges, gratuities, optional shore excursions and onboard personal purchases. Prizes are not transferable or redeemable for cash except as specified. No substitution for prizes except as necessary due to unavailability. Travel trailer and/or automobile license and registration fees are winners' responsibility as are any other incidental expenses not specified herein.

Early Bird Prize may not be offered in some presentations of this sweepstakes. Grand through third prize winners will have the option of selecting any prize offered at level won. All prizes will be awarded. Drawing will be held at 204 Center Square Road, Bridgeport, NJ 08014. Winners need not be present. For winners list (available in June, 1996), send a self-addressed, stamped envelope by 1/15/96 to: Dream Come True Winners, P.O. Box 572, Gibbstown, NJ 08027.

THE FOLLOWING APPLIES TO THE SWEEPSTAKES ABOVE:

No purchase necessary. No photocopied or mechanically reproduced entries will be accepted. Not responsible for lost, late, misdirected, damaged, incomplete, illegible, or postage-die mail. Entries become the property of sponsors and will not be returned.

Winner(s) will be notified by mail. Winner(s) may be required to sign and return an affidavit of eligibility/release within 14 days of date on notification or an alternate may be selected. Except where prohibited by law, entry constitutes permission to use of winners' names, hometowns, and likenesses for publicity without additional compensation. Void where prohibited or restricted. All federal, state, provincial, and local laws and regulations apply.

All prize values are in U.S. currency. Presentation of prizes may vary; values at a given prize level will be approximately the same. All taxes are winners' responsibility.

Canadian residents, in order to win, must first correctly answer a time-limited skill testing question administered by mail. Any litigation regarding the conduct and awarding of a prize in this publicity contest by a resident of the province of Quebec may be submitted to the Regie des loteries et courses du Quebec.

Sweepstakes is open to legal residents of the U.S., Canada, and Europe (in those areas where made available) who have received this offer.

Sweepstakes in sponsored by Ventura Associates, 1211 Avenue of the Americas, New York, NY 10036 and presented by independent businesses. Employees of these, their advertising agencies and promotional companies involved in this promotion, and their immediate families, agents, successors, and assignees shall be ineligible to participate in the promotion and shall not be eligible for any prizes covered herein.   SWP 3/95

DON'T MISS THESE FABULOUS
BANTAM WOMEN'S FICTION TITLES